I0623636

AMELIA
BATTLE FOR ARDENTIA

BROCK E. DESKINS

Amelia faced her foe without fear. Wind whipped her cobalt blue cape and golden hair behind her. The sun reflected off her silver breastplate, vambraces, and greaves so brightly that the light appeared to originate from the armor itself. She held her bronze shield before her with the embossed eagle on its face appearing as if it might leap forth and grab her enemy in its talons.

The figure before her stood in stark contrast to her radiant beauty. Romut was the specter of death and had been the bane of her existence for the past few years. With his black clothes, billowing cloak, and pale and withered flesh, he embodied pestilence and misery, seeking to spread the disease of his existence as far and wide as he could.

Only Amelia stood in his path, thwarting his corruption at every turn. With his back to a cliff, he had nowhere to flee. If you were to look at the pair squaring off, the matchup would appear ridiculous to the casual observer. A tall, powerful, evil sorcerer cringing in fear of a ten-year-old girl seemed preposterous, but Amelia was no mere child. She was a warrior princess, a demigoddess of light and purity who had sworn an oath to protect her world from evil.

Bolt after bolt of lightning arced from Romut's gnarly fingertips, but Amelia batted them aside with her shield and sword like a dual paddle-wielding, master ping-pong player and advanced. Romut took a shuffling step away from the furious warrior princess, but his foot reached the precipice overlooking a fertile valley and there was nowhere for him to go.

For Kellie M. Rahm
Sister, Daughter, Wife, Friend, Warrior.
(1969-2016)

PREFACE

Amelia: Battle for Ardentia, is a bit different than my usual genre of choice and people may wonder why I chose it. Amelia is a story of hope, love, joy, and tragedy. It is a fantasy that lives and breathes alongside our reality. For those who have ever stood helplessly by a sick loved one's side, it is a horror.

Fantasy has always been my escape. Growing up, I was no stranger to pain, and I do not refer to the scrapes, bruises, cuts, and broken bones common amongst adventurous and none too bright boys, but the emotional sort that cuts deep into one's very soul. I often felt weak and powerless in the real world, a victim who could not speak out much less fight back.

So, I created another world, many worlds, where I was far from helpless. In those worlds, I was a warrior, capable of amazing feats of strength and skill. I was a sorcerer who could harness awesome forces, not just in defense of myself but others. I was the hero for my conjured universe whom I so desperately needed in reality.

I think most people, if not all, create their own worlds at one time or another, places where they are accepted, loved, and do not suffer from any mortal frailties, physical or emotional. Amelia is sick and has been for a long time, even if no one, including herself, realized it, so she created a world where she was a warrior princess, a demigoddess, immune to fear and illness.

So, why did I write this story of reality and fantasy? When I was just a young child, cancer struck my mother, a few years before completing, my grandmother, and three years before the penning of this story, my sister. For three years, Kellie battled this horrible disease with a smile that hid her fear and a fiercely defiant scowl when faced with unbearable pain.

Her bravery and tenacity in the face of such a plight inspired me to write this story, not just for her but for everyone who has ever confronted true pain or evil and spat in its eye. So, this is for all the warrior princes and princesses out there. Kellie did not lose her battle with cancer; she simply went on to her next great adventure.

CHAPTER 1

A melia faced her foe without fear. Wind whipped her cobalt blue cape and golden hair behind her. The sun reflected off her silver breastplate, vambraces, and greaves so brightly that the light appeared to originate from the armor itself. She held her bronze shield before her with the embossed eagle on its face appearing as if it might leap forth and grab her enemy in its talons.

The figure before her stood in stark contrast to her radiant beauty. Romut was the specter of death and had been the bane of her existence for the past few years. With his black clothes, billowing cloak, and pale and withered flesh, he embodied pestilence and misery, seeking to spread the disease of his existence as far and wide as he could.

Only Amelia stood in his path, thwarting his corruption at every turn. With his back to a cliff, he had nowhere to flee. If you were to look at the pair squaring off, the matchup would appear ridiculous to the casual observer. A tall, powerful, evil sorcerer cringing in fear of a ten-year-old girl seemed preposterous, but Amelia was no mere child. She was a warrior princess, a demigoddess of light and purity who had sworn an oath to protect her world from evil.

Bolt after bolt of lightning arced from Romut's gnarly fingertips, but Amelia batted them aside with her shield and sword like a dual paddle-wielding, master ping-pong player and advanced. Romut took a shuffling step away from the furious warrior princess, but his foot reached the precipice overlooking a fertile valley and there was nowhere for him to go.

"Do you think this is the end?" Romut seethed, his voice grating like fingernails on a chalkboard. "Do you believe this is some fairy-tale where you triumph and everyone lives happily ever after?"

Amelia shot him a fierce glare. "No, this is Sparta!"

Her tiny foot came up and kicked him hard in the stomach. Romut shrieked a curse as he fell, one best not repeated by little girls, even demigoddesses. Amelia basked in her triumph, but black wings sprouted from Romut's back and stole away her joy.

"Technically, it was not Sparta, it was Englewood Park, and I was not supposed to have watched *300*, but it was such a cool movie! Anyway, that's what I did this summer," Amelia said as she stood before her fifth-grade class.

Mrs. Bernstrom, her teacher, gave her a lopsided smile and said, "That was a wonderful story, Amelia, but you were supposed to tell us what you *really* did on summer break."

"That's what I did!"

Bradley, sitting two rows back from the front of the class, rolled his eyes. "You are so weird. That's why you don't have any friends."

Amelia glared at her tormentor with the same intensity she had Romut. "I do too have friends, hundreds of them, entire cities and worlds of them!"

"You are so full of crap your eyes are brown."

"My eyes are blue!" Amelia shot back as she stalked back to her seat. "You're so full of crap your breath stinks."

The boy stuck out a foot and tripped her as she stormed by. She should have expected it, but her anger distracted her and she went sprawling.

Bradley chortled, "Demigoddess? More like demi-dork."

"Bradley, go to the principal's office!" Mrs. Bernstrom shouted.

His protest sounded over the laughter filling the classroom. "Why? I didn't do anything! She tripped over her own stupid feet."

Amelia scrambled to her hands and knees, ready to leap up and show Bradley what happened to people who sucker-punched a demigoddess, but she paused as she felt a drop of blood hang from the tip of her nose before falling and making a tiny red rain splatter on the floor. Another followed, and then it was as if someone had turned on a spigot.

"Um, Mrs. Bernstrom..." Amelia said in a shaky voice.

Her teacher began to walk toward her. "Amelia, are you okay? Amelia?"

Amelia was unable to answer as she swooned and her vision wavered. The teacher's and kids' voices sounded to her as if she were underwater. Blackness fell over her as if someone had turned out the lights for movie day, only it was even darker. She felt herself falling, but after what seemed like a full minute, she was still plunging into the darkness with no bottom in sight.

CHAPTER 2

A horrible clunking noise filled Amelia's ears. At first, she feared she was still trapped in the blackness that had overtaken her, but upon opening her eyes, she found her situation was far worse. White light surrounded her like a cocoon. She was trapped inside an opaque crystal coffin; the pounding was coming from her fists as she beat upon the walls and lid. She tried to lift her head but a sadistic mesh strap held her securely in place.

A hollow voice echoed through the sarcophagus. "Amelia, I need you to keep still."

"Romut? Let me go, you giant butthole!"

A softer, quavering voice resonated through the tiny chamber. "Amelia, sweetie, it's Mom. We're taking a picture, so you need to hold still."

Amelia's eyes flicked around the inside of the noisy MRI machine. "Oh. Should I smile?"

A trickle of laughter broke over the wall of pent-up fear in her mother's voice. "No, baby, that's okay. Just keep still. The doctor says we're almost done."

Amelia did as she was told and kept staring up at the white cylinder surrounding her. She had stopped hammering on the plastic interior, but the machine produced a great deal of banging noises all on its own. She thought back to her last fight with Romut and wondered if he had cast a spell on her and that was why she now found herself in this clanking contraption. Amelia wished she had kicked him between the legs instead of the stomach, but that's not what Leonidas had done, and if anyone knew how to kick a bad guy, it was Leonidas.

Besides, her father said she should not kick boys there after that time Bradley told on her when she kicked him in the crotch for calling her the B word. She tried to tell the principal and her parents that anyone who called a warrior princess the B word deserved to get kicked between the legs, but her defense fell on deaf ears, and she had to spend the next three recesses in the library. As if being forced to sit and read her favorite stories was some kind of punishment. Grown-ups. Go figure.

She felt herself sliding toward her feet and found that she was on a rolling slab of some kind. Long florescent lights and white ceiling panels replaced the plastic arch overhead. A man in a white lab coat unclipped the mesh mask trapping her head to the table and eased her up to a sitting position.

"Hello, Amelia. I'm Dr. Ingram. How do you feel?"

Amelia shrugged. "I have a headache, but I'm okay, I guess." She flicked her eyes toward her parents standing next to her and dropped her gaze to the floor. "Sorry for calling you a giant butthole. I thought you were someone else."

Dr. Ingram laughed and pushed his gold-rimmed glasses higher up his nose. "That's quite all right. I have been called far worse."

Amelia frowned and looked at her dad. "Have you looked him up on Yelp? If people are calling him names all the time, maybe we should find a better doctor."

She flashed a churlish smile as the grown-ups shared another laugh, her parents putting effort into theirs to hide the anxiety they felt. Despite their efforts, her parents' faces resumed their somber appearance, their smiles dragged down by the gravity of Amelia's situation.

Dr. Ingram put his hand on her back. "Can you stand up?"

Amelia hopped off the table and tried to hide the slight swoon she felt upon landing. "Of course I can. I can do a backflip if you want me to."

Despite her bravado, the doctor lowered her into a waiting wheelchair. "Seeing you go after my MRI machine; I have no doubt you could."

Amelia snorted. "You're lucky I didn't have my sword, or I would have chopped that thing to bits."

"Well then, I'm glad you left that at home. I don't think either of us could afford to replace it."

Amelia pressed her lips into a thin line. "You're probably right. Being a warrior princess is great, and the people love me, but the job doesn't pay squat. Look at me. I still rely on my parents' insurance plan."

"Maybe you should unionize," Dr. Ingram suggested.

She rolled her eyes. "Have you seen my people? Getting a bunch of demigods and goddesses to work together is like trying to form the world's first all-cat swim team. We are a contrary bunch."

The doctor chuckled as he pushed Amelia out of the room and down the hall. Her parents kept pace on each side of her wheelchair, constantly looking over and reaching down to touch her head or shoulder as if afraid she might suddenly disappear. Amelia found it more than a little annoying.

"Mr. and Mrs. Poole, please have a seat," Dr. Ingram said as he ushered Amelia's parents into his office.

"Dan and Linda, please," Amelia's dad replied.

"How bad is it?" Linda blurted out, unable to contain her fear.

Dr. Ingram grimaced and began displaying MRI images on a large monitor. "It's not good, I'm afraid."

Linda clutched Dan's hand hard enough to bring pain and leaned into his shoulder.

"Amelia has a substantial growth in her brain. We call it pediatric glioma. Pediatric gliomas are tumors that form in or between the thalamus and hypothalamus."

Dan and Linda's world shattered in an instant. The floor felt as if it had opened and swallowed them whole, pulling them down into the darkest pit of Hell. The anguished wails surrounding them were not from a multitude of tortured souls but their own silent, desperate cries of denial.

Dan caught his breath, coughed once to clear his throat, and asked, "You're sure? There is no way this could be something else, something benign? Maybe some kind of anomaly in the image, or maybe the MRI is defective."

Dr. Ingram shook his head. "It is very clear what we are dealing with. I wish it were something else, anything else really."

"What exactly does this mean?" Linda asked.

"The hypothalamus helps regulate sleep, and damage to it can cause visual or auditory anomalies. Has Amelia shown any signs of odd behavior, particularly seeing things that aren't there or said anything about unusually vivid dreams, maybe even while she's awake?"

Linda cast a worried look at Dan. "She has always had a powerful imagination and makes up these wild stories. She's been doing it almost since she could talk."

Dr. Ingram nodded. "Do these stories always include a giant butthole by the name of Romut?"

Dan chuckled despite the serious situation. "He has been her archenemy for about three years now, some evil wizard who is set on destroying the demigoddess warrior princess."

Linda clamped a hand over her mouth. "I should have seen this. What kind of mother doesn't know when her child is sick? I should have had her in here years ago!"

Dr. Ingram set a chair in front of the couple and sat down. "These fantasies of hers could be nothing more than the active imagination of a very clever girl and have nothing to do with her condition. Has she had any other symptoms, like headaches or balance problems?"

Dan shook his head. "She leaps around like a crazed monkey all day long."

"She has mentioned headaches a few times," Linda said. "They didn't sound severe and they weren't frequent. My only concern was that she might have inherited my migraines. Why didn't I see this?" she snapped, slamming her hand against the chair's armrest.

"No one is to blame," Dr. Ingram assured her. "It is simply one of the more terrible things that happen in life, and it is just bad luck that it happened to Amelia. I know this doesn't make it any better, but I have had to talk to parents far too many times about something like this. They all feel guilty, in that they should have done something different or sooner, but the guilt is misplaced and does not help anyone get better. We can only act on what we now face."

"What do we do?" Dan asked, his tone pleading for the doctor to tell them that he could cure their daughter.

Dr. Ingram leaned back and let out a long breath. "The tumor's location all but eliminates surgical or radiation treatment. I certainly wouldn't perform such an operation here. I recommend we start chemotherapy immediately in hopes of shrinking the mass."

"And if that doesn't work?"

"I'm going to contact the Dana-Farber Boston Children's Cancer and Blood Disorders Center and see if I can get Amelia on their list. Dana-Farber has the top pediatric glioma program in the nation."

"What will they do there?" Linda asked.

"They have immediate access to trials or surgical options if the chemo is unsuccessful."

"And you don't think the chemo will work?"

"We should be prepared for all eventualities. Time is not on our side, and any delay may be costly."

Linda swallowed and looked down at her clenched fists. "Prepared for all eventualities…"

"I won't lie to either of you. Amelia's condition is severe and her prognosis is not favorable. That does not mean that anything is a forgone conclusion, only that we all are going to have a tough fight ahead of us."

Linda looked to her husband. "What do we tell Amelia?"

Dr. Ingram interjected. "My usual approach, and knowing Amelia for the short time I have, I would suggest honesty."

Linda choked back a sob. "She is just a girl."

"Children are more resilient than we give them credit for, and in dealing with things like this, they are often stronger than we adults are."

Amelia turned her head at the sound of her door opening and watched her parents and Dr. Ingram walk in bearing dour expressions.

"Why so sad, Dad? Why so glum, Mum? Why so gloomy, roomie? Um…, why the blues, dudes?"

Her parents pressed against her hospital bed, and her mom gripped her hand. "Oh, baby, I'm so sorry!"

Amelia looked to her dad, knowing she would not be able to talk to her mom when she was like this. "Geez, who died?"

Her dad used his left arm to support her mom while he stroked Amelia's hair with the other. "Sweetheart, you are very sick."

"I am? I don't feel sick. Is that why I passed out?"

"It is."

"What's wrong with me?"

Dan looked to Dr. Ingram, who gave him a nod and said, "You have a tumor in your brain."

Although only ten years old, Amelia understood what her dad was saying. Television and the Internet made children far more educated about complex topics than they probably should be, and she knew the gravity of having a tumor in her brain. She also knew this was going to be terrible for her parents, so she forced down her fear and responded the best way she knew how—with humor.

Amelia frowned and spoke in her best Arnold Schwarzenegger voice. "It's not a tooma!"

Linda's knees buckled but she caught herself with Dan's help. "I can't do this!" she said, then fled from the room.

Amelia watched her mom dart out of the room and looked at her dad. "Geez, just because it was a bad movie doesn't mean it wasn't a good joke."

"She's just not in the mood for jokes right now, honey."

"There's a surprise! I think I'm going to have a heart attack and die from not surprise!"

"Don't you mean that surprise?"

"Are you seriously questioning me about movie quotes?"

Dan smiled and patted his daughter's leg. "You're right. I should know better."

Amelia turned her eyes to Dr. Ingram. "So, what's up, doc? What do we do? Open up my skull and use an ice-cream scoop to dig out this tooma?"

The doctor rested his hand against her bed railing. "We'll write that up as plan B. We are going to start giving you some medicine that will hopefully kill the…tooma."

"You mean chemo?"

"Exactly. I must warn you that it will probably make you very sick, and you might lose your beautiful hair."

Amelia grabbed a lock of her long hair and sighed. "Well, as long as I get superpowers in the end then I can handle it."

Dr. Ingram chuckled. "I can't promise you any superpowers."

She turned a fierce glare on her dad. "See, I told you we should have checked this guy out on Yelp! Go find me a mad scientist with questionable ethics who's willing to shoot me full of mutagen so I can become a superhero."

"I think Dr. Ingram has a good handle on this, so we should stick with him. Besides, none of the mad scientists are in our insurance network."

"Probably because you were too cheap to spring for the gold package. But no, *silver is good enough for my family. We don't need mutagen.* Bet you feel pretty dumb now."

Dan smiled and squeezed her hand. "I sure do. Get some rest, kiddo. I need to go talk to your mom."

Amelia held her dad's hand tighter, the playful defiance slipping from her face. "Daddy, am I going to be okay?"

Dan looked up at the ceiling and tried to block the tears threatening to escape by squeezing his eyes closed. He clenched his jaw in an effort to still its trembling. "Of course you are, sweetheart. You're my warrior princess."

"Can you do something for me?"

"Of course, baby. What is it?"

"If I die, can you put Deadpoole on my tombstone instead of Amelia Poole?"

It was too much. Dan covered his face with his hands and wiped away the tears before answering in a shuddering voice. "Absolutely not, and you better not watch that movie."

Amelia looked away. "Okay, I will not watch that movie in future."

"Amelia, I mean it."

"I said I promise not to watch it!" She twisted her head and pushed the end of her pillow against her mouth. "Again."

"What was that?"

"What was what?"

"What did you say into your pillow?"

"Nothing, I just burped. Excuse me for having manners."

Dan reached down and held his daughter. "I love you, sweetie."

"Love you too, Daddy."

CHAPTER 3

A melia strode through the blackened forest, her footsteps creating small, grey clouds around her feet with every impact. Heat washed over her from the glowing embers hidden beneath the ash and made her break out in a sweat. Burnt trees loomed all around her like charred skeletons that refused to fall to the ravages of the fire that had swept through the land. There was no life in the formerly verdant forest. She was alone, the animals that once inhabited the woods having fled before the flames or succumbed to them.

An orange glow limned the hills ahead of her where the inferno continued its reign of destruction. Fighting forest fires was not normally within the purview of warrior princesses, but this was no ordinary blaze. The flames were deliberate, calculating, and moved with evil intent. Only one creature was so foul and wantonly destructive—Romut.

Sulfur and smoke burned her lungs and assaulted her senses as Amelia scaled the hill and drew nearer to the source of destruction. When she finally crested the hilltop, she gazed down at the form Romut had taken and gasped. Amelia immediately regretted the involuntary act as she started coughing and choking on the fetid air.

A wave of nausea sent ripples through her stomach. Romut was a titan made of stone and magma. Like a living volcano, he set the forest ablaze and turned any water into yellow sludge that steamed and hissed at his touch.

Amelia knew her sword, powerful and blessed to combat evil, was woefully insufficient for the enormity of the task before her. Leaving the glimmering blade in its sheath, she unslung her bow, knocked a silvery arrow, and let it fly.

The arrow streaked across the expanse separating Amelia from her foe and lodged in Romut's shoulder. The attack seemed paltry, the shaft sticking out of the titanic monster like a bee's stinger, but he roared with outrage and turned to unleash his fury and destruction upon Amelia.

Romut reeled back one massive arm and whipped it forward as if to swat the pesky insect despite being too far away to reach her. Amelia's eyes went wide when a magma-like glob detached from the limb and flew at her with the speed and accuracy of a Major League pitch. Amelia leapt back and slid down the slope she had just climbed, narrowly missing being hit by the world's nastiest dodgeball.

The giant globule struck the ridge where she had been standing with a thunderous yet squelching slap, like hurling a handful of wet clay onto the sidewalk. Gravel, dirt, and fist-sized blobs of magma rained down around her.

Amelia discovered that the lava's fiery heat was not the only danger Romut's attack presented. Everywhere the globes struck, they raised noxious clouds that reeked of sulfur and sickness. Every breath caused Amelia's lungs to burn and her eyes to water, and made her sick to her stomach.

The warrior princess fought back the toxic effects through force of will and scrambled along the slope until she was able to get Romut back in her sights. She unleashed a volley of arrows, every one of them striking home. Romut returned her assault by flinging flaming pestilence at her from his fingertips, but Amelia did not wait around to suffer its effects. She scurried away as fast as her legs would take her, loosing arrows on the run, her aim never faltering.

Romut lunged forward with startling speed and slammed a giant fist down. Amelia barely managed to dodge the blow by leaping to the side and rolling down into a ravine. The air turned toxic and she could barely see through the tears pouring from her eyes. Amelia's breath came in rasping coughs as her lungs burned and her stomach heaved.

"I will crush you, you pathetic little bug," Romut said, his voice gurgling with laughter as a second blow crushed and scorched the ground Amelia had just vacated.

A dozen pithy responses flashed through her mind, but she was unable to utter them due to the sickening conflict raging inside her body. Amelia scrambled to her feet and ran down the gorge as fast as she could go, but Romut stayed just behind her, smashing his car-sized fists against the ground with every other step. She slid to a stop when the path ended at a cliff overlooking the ocean. Amelia cast her eyes and head about for a way to escape, but Romut removed any choice she might have had.

His fist came crashing down, and the ground beneath her feet shattered. The cliff edge broke off in a large slab accompanied by a shower of rubble. Amelia shrieked as she plummeted toward the sea, a fall that seemed to take forever despite how quickly the water rushed up toward her.

She pushed off the boulder upon which she was riding and launched herself farther out into the water in hopes of missing the jagged rocks at the base of the cliff. Amelia could hear Romut's laughter until she struck the water, and then she heard nothing more.

Romut studied the roiling ocean for a full minute, ready to sling putrescent lava at the demigoddess the moment she bobbed to the surface. Only the waves disturbed the smooth swells before they broke upon the rocks. The creature of death and devastation turned away to resume his destruction.

He spun back around at the sound of a particularly large wave crashing against the cliff—only it was not a wave. A colossal sea serpent burst from the ocean depths, its serpentine body rising over the cliff face high enough to meet Romut's gaze. Romut's look of surprise turned to fury when he spotted the small figure, her silver armor shining, perched atop the creature's head.

"Time for you to die!" Amelia shouted.

"Stupid child, you cannot destroy me."

Romut swung his arm back to unleash another assault, but Amelia's new friend was faster. The sea serpent opened its mouth wide and spewed forth a blast of water with the volume and intensity of an opened fire hydrant. The geyser struck Romut in the chest and drove him back.

Amelia held tight to a pair of horns jutting from the creature's head as it dove beneath the waves and sucked in another tanker truck's worth of water. Amelia and her pet rose up once more and unleashed a second aqueous attack, knocking Romut from his feet with a thunderous crash. Steam roiled off the toxic titan as the water struck and hardened his "skin," causing great chunks of stone, and whatever else his abominable conjuring was made of, to slough off.

Like the Wicked Witch of the West in *The Wizard of Oz*, Romut melted under the assault. Amelia and her serpent refused to relent until they had washed away every trace of him. Despite her success, she knew it was unlikely she had destroyed him. This was but another battle in a long war.

A knock sounded at the bathroom door. "Amelia, honey, are you all right?" her mother asked as she opened the door.

Amelia looked up from where her cheek rested against the cool surface of the toilet seat. "This sucks more than anything that has ever sucked before."

Linda knelt next to her daughter and rubbed her back. "I'm so sorry, sweetie. I know it's awful. I would do anything to take your place."

Amelia smiled despite her misery. "Go for it. There's plenty of toilet for everyone."

For Amelia, her greatest foe was Romut, an evil force no one fully understood beyond his desire to destroy everything in his sight. Although his touch withered the body and could sap a person's very soul, it was a physical thing and could thus be battled. It was tangible. Weapons could be forged that would do him harm and, if one was lucky, destroy him, or at least drive him from the body.

For those who stood beside their sick loved ones, there was a far more sinister foe, one that could not be seen but whose destructive presence was undeniable and unavoidable. That evil's name was hope. Hope that the next treatment would free their loved one from Romut's grip. Hope that a cure was just around the corner. Hope that they would wake up and recognize their nightmare for the phantasm it was, a bad dream plaguing their night-time fantasies. Hope that their loved one would wake up whole, healthy, and happy. Hope was almost close enough to touch but always remained just a hair's breadth out of reach.

That was the evil Amelia's parents battled every minute of every day. It was a war in which they lost ground inch by inch, but neither of them would yield to it no matter how inevitable the outcome. They did not fight for themselves; they fought for something far more precious, something for which they would die a thousand times over if just to carry on the fight for one more day—their precious Amelia.

Dan and Linda waited in Dr. Ingram's office, a place they had learned to despise. It was where hope lived and died. It lifted their spirits only to dash them upon the rocks of despair days or even weeks later. It was a rollercoaster ride whose arcs rose into the heavens before dropping them into the deepest pits of hell.

Dr. Ingram sat behind his desk with his fingers interlaced, a sign the parents had learned to recognize as bad news. "Amelia's latest treatment has been less than effective. The chemo has not gotten us where I'd like us to be. There has been some reduction in size, but I would have liked to have seen more."

"What now?" Dan asked.

"I have secured a place for her at Dana-Farber in Boston. I also took the liberty of reserving a suite at the Grand Gloucester. It is a nice hotel not far from the clinic, and they cater to extended stays for situations like yours. Your insurance should have no problem covering the cost. Of course, you are welcome to make your own arrangements if you like, assuming that this is the route you want to take."

"What are our options?" Linda asked.

"Honestly, there aren't many. There are other treatments available, but I think Dana-Farber is Amelia's best hope. I have put together a package with information about the other trials, but I think you will agree that Boston is the best option. Feel free to talk it over or consult with another oncologist. We have to take big steps, and these are important choices to make."

CHAPTER 4

A melia sat astride her powerful war horse and adjusted the lance and shield in her hands as she stared at her foe across the jousting lane. The Black Knight set himself in the saddle and fought to control his anxious destrier while holding onto his weapon. He was the greatest knight in the mortal realm, and he was here to prove he was the best in the immortal world as well.

"You made a big mistake challenging me, Black Knight," Amelia called out. "It is not too late for you to concede."

"You speak the words of someone who is afraid, Warrior Princess," the Black Knight returned. "I am the hero of these people, not you, and I will prove it on the field of battle."

Amelia lowered her lance. "So be it."

The Black Knight lowered his in response, readied his shield, and spurred his mount. The two horses raced forward, hurtling their riders to an inevitable collision of wood, steel, and flesh. The warriors met in the middle of the field with a resounding crash. Lances struck shields, the impact rocking both riders back in their saddles.

"What are you kids doing?" a nurse shrieked from down the hall.

Amelia and Jayden rested their lances made from a pair of crutches padded with bath towels across their laps and spun their wheelchairs around to face the irate nurse.

"Jousting," Amelia replied as if the answer were obvious.

"You are going to hurt yourselves! How would I explain that to your parents?"

Amelia raised her bedpan shield and tapped it against her bedpan helmet. "We wore protective gear! Safety first, that's what I always say."

The nurse was about to respond, but Dr. Ingram and Amelia's parents rounded the corner. Her mom frowned and her dad rolled his eyes, not surprised in the least to find her causing trouble.

"What's up, doc?" she asked as Dr. Ingram grabbed the handles on the back of her wheelchair.

"We need to talk about your treatment," he replied as he began pushing her down the hall.

"How do you feel?" her mom asked.

"Not bad. I only barfed twice today."

"I guess that's good—oh, what is that smell?" Linda asked as she fanned the air in front of her face.

Amelia sniffed her bedpan shield. "It might be my barf pan, but I thought I washed it. Oh, wait, sorry, that was me. Chemo fart." She looked over her shoulder at Dr. Ingram. "Hey, maybe that's my superpower? Gas Girl!"

"Amelia," her mom said in a scolding tone.

"Oh, how about Drive By? That's the one! Not the coolest ability, but I'll take what I can get."

"Later, Amelia," Jayden, aka the Black Knight, said as she rolled past him.

"Later, Tater."

Jayden's hand flew over his nose. "Amelia!"

Amelia gave him a sinister laugh. "Hashtag drive by!"

Dan looked down at her with a forced scowl. "Amelia..."

She placed her hand over her stomach and whimpered, "I'm sick, Daddy, I can't help it."

"That was a line from Deadpool."

"It was?" she asked in feigned innocence. "Must be some kind of crazy coincidence."

"Uh-huh."

It did not take long for her parents to come to a decision. They studied the treatment information and consulted with other doctors, and nearly every one advised them to take Amelia to Boston. So, Boston it was. Amelia was excited. She had never been on an airplane before.

Through the terminal windows, she watched the enormous aircraft take off and land with rapt attention. She could not believe how many people were packed into Denver's airport, all waiting to board a plane. One good thing about being sick and bedecked in her "chemo clothes," was she did not have to suffer the long lines as the other passengers did.

Amelia was just glad they let her walk onto the plane. She had had enough of wheelchairs in the hospital. If her purple headwrap did not display her condition, the surgical mask covering her face left no room for doubt.

She received plenty of sympathetic smiles whenever she met anyone's eyes, enough so that she felt like running them through with her sword. She was a warrior princess, and warrior princesses were to be feared and respected, not pitied.

"Do you want to sit next to the window?" her mom asked as they made their way to their seats.

"No thanks. I should sit in the aisle in case I need to get to the bathroom."

"Are you sure? It's a nice day and you'll be able to see some really great scenery."

"I'm fine."

Besides, Amelia knew the best scenery in the world was inside her head. She watched the people stream onto the plane after her, nearly all of them staring at her while trying to make it look as though they weren't.

Amelia looked up at the speaker as the captain announced that they were ready for takeoff. Minutes later, the plane rolled forward, the engines whined, and Amelia smiled as an invisible force pushed her back into her seat.

"Whoa-ho!" Amelia yelped as she looked across the seats to the window and at the ground dropping away beneath them.

"I told you to sit by the window," her mom said as Amelia leaned over her lap to see.

Amelia did not respond; instead, she leaned back in her seat, closed her eyes, and enjoyed the wind blowing against her face. She marveled at how fast they were flying, but an airship had to be fast to catch a dragon. She peered out over the rail, only her tight grip on a nearby rope keeping her from plunging over the side and falling thousands of feet.

"Princess," Captain Donoghue called out, "would you mind not leaning out over the abyss? I'd rather not lose you overboard, especially if we do manage to catch that scaly beast."

Amelia pulled herself back in and walked across the deck to the captain. The ship looked like something out of *Pirates of the Caribbean*, as did her crew. The only real difference was that this one flew through the sky instead of sailing on the sea. She let out a whoop and caught herself when the airship bucked from air turbulence.

"No worries, Captain. I'm as steady as a barge in a bathtub," Amelia replied. "Any sign of our dragon yet?"

The captain opened his mouth to respond, but the lookout high in the crow's nest answered for him. "We got something a few degrees off the port bow. It's got wings!"

Captain Donoghue let out a long breath, his face pale. "I hope you're ready, Princess." He shouted out to his crew, "Steady ahead! Man the ballistae!"

Men wearing canvas trousers and little else scurried across the deck, loaded the powerful siege weapons, and armed themselves with long spears and powerful crossbows. Amelia gripped her golden bow in her hand and raced for the prow, desperate to be the first to engage the frightening beast that had been terrorizing villages for weeks.

They were not far from the town of Windlow, likely the dragon's next victim. The beast spotted the airship and dipped its wings, banked back around, and headed straight for them. Amelia loosed a silver arrow the moment the dragon was close enough for her to make out the larger, individual scales.

The dragon roared its fury when the silver dart pierced its rock-hard hide and dug deep into its flesh. It veered aside just as it released a massive gout of flame, its deviation sparing many men their lives.

Crossbows and their much larger brethren twanged and spat metal-tipped slivers after the dragon. Some struck home and breached the tough scales, but only just, and not many at that. The dragon screeched again, more out of insult than pain, its blaring rebuke promising death.

Amelia sprinted across the deck to keep her eyes and deadly bow trained on the dragon as it flew off and looped back for another pass. The ship turned to give chase, but while fast, it was not nearly as dexterous as the dragon was.

More arrows streaked from Amelia's bow like tiny lightning bolts as the dragon made another run at the ship. Undeterred, its huge mouth opened up and spat fire. Amelia and the men around her dropped to the deck. Only the shield strapped across her back saved her from the creature's fiery breath. The cries around her showed that others were not as fortunate.

The dragon circled around for a third pass. Amelia loosed three arrows in rapid succession, forcing the dragon to dive below the ship. She cast her bow down, sprinted across the deck, and drew her fantastic sword as she leapt over the rail. Amelia fell far, but not too far for a demigoddess. Her feet struck the dragon hard and she stumbled to catch her balance.

The dragon craned its head around on its long neck and snarled, showing off its many sharp teeth. It dipped its left wing and banked, turning its back almost vertical to the ground. Amelia parted her legs and straddled the beast's neck, locking herself in place just like she did when riding horses bareback.

She wedged her hand beneath a large scale as the dragon completely inverted, turning her upside down. Amelia was certain she was going to fall, but the dragon rolled upright as it was unable to maintain flight while upside down.

With no other recourse, Amelia raised her blade and plunged it into the great dragon's neck. The beast cried out and began to fall. Instinct took over and it locked its wings as Amelia rode the creature to the ground in a long, winding spiral. She held tightly onto her sword as the creature struck the ground hard just on the outskirts of Windlow.

The dragon's huge, cat-like eyes rolled back to look at her and spoke in Romut's voice. "You have won the battle yet again, but you will lose this war." The colossal beast let out a shuddering breath and lay still.

Frightened townsfolk streamed from the village and surrounded her, some cheering and clapping, others simply looking on in either horror or calm detachment.

Amelia raised her sword over her head. "Fear not, people, for I have slain the dragon!"

"That's nice, honey, but I really need you to get off the cart so I can finish serving drinks."

Amelia looked around the cabin as she straddled the drink cart, a rolled-up airline magazine gripped in her hand and held over her head. The flight attendant stood behind her, several paper wrappers from the arsenal of straws Amelia had taken from McDonald's during their lunch sticking out of her hair.

Amelia flashed the people in the cabin a sheepish grin. "Oops, sorry."

Dan reached over the seatback, lifted Amelia from the cart, and plunked her down in front of him. "I think we can do without the warrior princess for the rest of the flight."

"Queen."

"What?"

"I'm a warrior queen now."

"Since when?"

Amelia rolled her eyes. "Everyone knows you level up if you slay a dragon. Duh."

"My mistake, but I don't think we need any more saving today."

CHAPTER 5

Boston was not much different than Denver. The tall buildings blooming overhead were similar even if some stood higher than anything she had seen back home. The air certainly smelled different, and not in a good way. The city's backdrop was downright boring; absent were the mountains reaching up to give the sky some contour.

The cab dropped them off in front of a tall building. A man in a uniform opened the door for them as her dad pushed a cart loaded down with their luggage. Amelia gazed up at the glittering chandeliers suspended from the hotel's high ceiling.

She shifted her gaze to the floor that was so shiny she could see her muted reflection in its surface. She hopscotched across the alternating tile colors until she got too tired and followed her parents to the long counter, pausing only a moment to take in the fountain in the middle of the lobby gurgling promises of adventure. Those would have to wait for now.

"Daniel Poole," her dad said to the man behind the counter. "We have a reservation."

The desk clerk tapped on a computer keyboard. "Mr. Poole, we have your suite ready. I see you are staying with us for a while. There is a kitchen in your room, or we have a restaurant just off the lobby. I can have someone bring your luggage to your room if you like."

"That would be great, thank you," Dan replied.

The clerk handed him a pair of key cards. "These are for your room and will also grant you entrance to the laundry facilities and the gym. Enjoy your stay."

Dan took the key cards, handed one to Linda, and left their luggage for the bellhop to attend to, except for their carry-on bags. Amelia, somewhat rested, hopscotched behind her parents to the elevator. She smiled at the elderly black man wearing a red and gold uniform, standing in the far corner of the car.

He returned her smile, his white teeth in stark contrast to his dark skin. "Would you like to push the button?"

Amelia looked to her dad. "Can I, Dad?"

"Can you what?"

"Push the button."

"Sure. It's number fourteen."

The button lit up at Amelia's touch and the elevator drifted upward almost silently.

"Very well done," the elevator operator said. "You have a real knack for the job. My name is Otis."

"Amelia," she responded.

"Very nice to meet you, Amelia."

Linda looked down at her daughter. "Who are you talking to, sweetie?"

Otis grinned and pressed a wrinkled finger to his lips.

Amelia bit her lower lip to hide her mischievous smile. "No one."

The elevator came to a stop and the doors whooshed open.

"You should come back and see me when you can," Otis said as Amelia and her parents stepped out. "I've worked here a long time, and I can show you many wonderful things."

"Okay."

"Okay what?" her mom asked.

Amelia looked back at Otis, who gave her a wink as the doors closed behind them. "Nothing."

"Amelia, please, no warrior princess in the hotel," her mother pleaded. "We don't want to disturb the other guests."

"I'm a warrior queen now. Don't you remember the dragon?"

Linda rolled her eyes and sighed. "I remember the dragon. Over a hundred people on that airplane will never forget about the dragon."

"Yeah, it was an epic battle."

"Just...no dragons or wizards or whatever inside the hotel. We'll find a park or something nearby and you can slay all the evil you want there."

"I'll try, but evil is kind of known for breaking rules. It's pretty much the definition of evil."

"Amelia, I mean it," her mom said.

Amelia raised her hands and let them drop to her sides. "Fine, if they show up, I'll ask them to take it outside."

Linda closed her eyes and rubbed her temples.

"Are you all right?" Dan asked.

"I think I have a migraine coming on. I thought I might with the cabin pressure and all."

Dan slid the key card through the lock and opened the door. "Go lie down. We could probably all use a nap."

"Daddy, can I go explore the hotel?"

"Absolutely not," her mother answered.

"But I'm bored!"

"You've been here five minutes."

"Time is very conceptual."

Her dad snorted. "Where did you hear that?"

"*Cosmos*. I think Neil deGrasse Tyson knows what he's talking about."

Linda groaned. "Especially if he has children."

Amelia ran to the window and looked out across the city. "Did you hear that?"

"Hear what?" her dad asked.

"It sounded like a dragon's roar. Maybe it was just a car horn...maybe."

"Perhaps your dad can show you around the hotel."

Amelia rolled her eyes. "Right, because exploring isn't fun unless your parents are around."

Linda threw up her hands. "Fine, go play in the hall, but be quiet, and take my phone with you so you can reach us if anything happens or we need to call you back. Do not leave the hotel and do not go into anyone's room!"

Amelia batted her eyes. "Even if they have candy?"

"Yes, even if—do you want me to change my mind?"

Amelia ran to the table where her mom had laid her purse, took out the cell phone, and sprinted toward the door. "Later taters!"

Linda watched her daughter flee the room. "How can a girl that sick have so much energy?"

Dan shrugged. "Children aren't human."

Amelia raced down the hallway toward the elevator at the end. The doors opened at her approach as if expecting her. Otis stood waiting inside with a broad smile plastered across his face.

"Back so soon?" he asked as Amelia literally jumped inside the car.

"Yep." She looked around the elevator car, her eyes locking onto a brass plate below the buttons. "Hey, you have your name on the elevator."

Otis chuckled. "Different Otis."

"Why couldn't my mom and dad see you?"

"I'm only here for very special people."

Amelia nodded. "Ah, because I'm a warrior queen."

Otis touched his index finger to the side of his nose and pointed it at her. "Exactly. So, where would you like to go?"

Amelia shrugged. "I don't know. You're the hotel expert. You pick a floor."

"Oh, I haven't been that kind of elevator operator for a long time. I don't take people between floors; I take them to where they truly want to go."

"Like where?"

"Wherever you wish in time or space or somewhere in between."

Amelia sucked in a long gasp. "Oh. My. God! Is this a Tardis?"

Otis gave her a wink and a smile. "It's better than a Tardis."

She touched the phone in her back pocket. "I sure hope they have cell reception there or my mom's gonna freak."

CHAPTER 6

The ship's deck rolled beneath Amelia's feet as sea spray misted her face every time the bow plunged into the rolling ocean swells. It was a large vessel built for war, but the endless, unrelenting power of the vast sea tossed it about as if it were a toy.

Tales of pirates raiding merchant vessels had spread throughout the kingdom of late, but that was not why Amelia was aboard the *Excelsior*. Her prey was far more dangerous than a bunch of scruffy, smelly pirates.

Monsters prowled these waters, and Amelia was here to put an end to them. While seafaring merchants spread stories of pirates looting their valuable cargo, no such tales of monsters reached the ears of the King or even other merchants within the guild halls or taverns, for there were none left alive who witnessed such horrors to speak of them. Only a holy missive Amelia received gave credence to the rumors.

The ship's captain stood next to Amelia. Unlike the warrior queen, he forewent any handhold to steady his balance on the rolling deck. A tall man, he loomed over the comparatively diminutive girl, but his tone and expression were devoid of judgement or disdain for the success of his mission lying on a girl's tiny shoulders.

Captain Farthing looked like a man more suited to galas and attending royal court than a ship's captain. Hansome, lean, and muscular, and in his forties, he was the opposite of the salty seadog one would typically associate with the position.

"Rough seas and no sightings of ship nor sail for days," Captain Farthing said with his gaze locked on the same horizon as Amelia's.

"Do you think we're on a wild goose chase?" Captain Lancette, commander of the Special Royal Guard, asked.

Captain Lancette, unlike the ship's captain, appeared every inch the noble officer for the prestigious position he held. Of average height and a swordsman's build, he was young, blond-haired, and sported a patrician's angled nose.

Captain Farthing pressed his lips together and gave him a grim nod. "Looking that way."

Amelia shook her head. "No. They're close. I can feel their scorn and hatred."

Captain farthing swiveled his head around. "Not to be contrary, Highness, but despite the rough seas, we've a clear line of sight for miles. At least when we reach the apex of one of these mountainous swells. If they're within hours of us, we'd see them."

Amelia turned a full circle in frustration, scanning every inch of the sea around them. She furrowed her brow. "Unless we're looking in the wrong direction."

Captain Lancette gazed skyward. "Unless they are riding atop giant birds or dragons, I know not where else they might be."

"No, not flying," Amelia said as she stared at the deck beneath her feet.

Captain Farthing opened his mouth to speak, but it fell open even farther as he gaped at the freakish vessel that breached like a whale in a massive spray of water just off their starboard rail. The ship was a monstrosity of timber that looked to have been salvaged from various shipwrecks, all held together with coral and barnacles.

Hideous fish-like creatures clung to the sides and crowded its deck. They clutched harpoons and spears made of coral or rusty cutlasses likely salvaged from the crews of the sunken ships that now comprised their own vessel.

"Hard to port!" Captain Farthing shouted.

Several voices repeated the command, and the helmsman swung the bow away from the strange ship intent upon ramming them. The deck lurched beneath Amelia's feet and she clung tighter to the line she held in her small but vice-like grip to keep from being flung into the angry sea.

A terribly loud crunch and scraping sound filled everyone's ears as the timber and coral ship scraped hard against *Excelsior's* hull. While timbers creaked and cracked and coral sheared off the attacking vessel, they were able to avoid a direct collision, and the *Excelsior* managed to shake off the worst of the damage.

Captain Lancette drew his longsword and shouted, "To arms! We're being boarded! Fight for your lives, lads. There will be no quarter nor surrendered asked nor offered this day!"

More than sailors comprised the *Excelsior's* crew. Captain Lancette commanded nearly a full company of royal knights. And while they had exchanged their heavy steel armor for lighter brigandine they could quickly shrug off should they find themselves in the water, every officer was a royal marine, adept at fighting on land or sea.

If the creatures had thought to sack another vulnerable merchant ship this day, they were in for a very painful and costly surprise. The fact that Amelia was aboard as well likely spelled their inevitable doom.

Weapons clashed, and the curses of both men and monster filled the air. The two captains stepped forward with weapons drawn to protect the warrior queen, but Amelia was no maiden needing the protection of men.

Her sword glowed with righteous power as she slipped between the two officers. Crescents of golden light tracked along the path of every swing as she hewed down any monster foolish enough to get near or draw her attention.

Despite her presence and the battle-hardened crew, the fishmen pirates seemed endless. No matter how many they cut down, more streamed from the coral ship and sea to take their place. The vessel seemed more of a giant mother, birthing endless numbers of her spawn, than a ship.

The crew, and even Amelia, found themselves being slowly but steadily pushed back and pressed against *Excelsior's* rails. She knew she needed to change the tide of the battle and quickly.

Amelia hated to use her trump card, but as the creatures laid low more of the knights and sailors, she had little choice. Pointing her sword at the heavens, she beseeched the goddess of light and life for her divine blessing to cleanse the foulness besetting them all.

The clouds parted and golden rays of sunlight streamed down. The multitude of diffused beams converged into several spotlights as if to illuminate multiple actors on a stage.

Only these spotlights did more than simply highlight the many proverbial players. Any fishman caught within its luminous caress burned like ants under a magnifying glass while healing the wounds of Amelia's allies.

A large ray of light struck the coral ship, its beam slicing through its center and sending the two halves back into the murky depths whence it came. Any fish folk not scorched into a blackened husk leapt overboard and followed their ruined vessel to the ocean floor.

Loud cheers of HUZZAH! roared across the deck even as the soldiers and sailors tended to the wounded.

"I have to say, that was the most horrible and perilous battle I have ever been in," Captain Lancette said between gasping breaths.

"Aye," Captain Farthing croaked out.

Amelia stood silent and stock still, her senses spreading out across the sea and plumbing the murky depths. The surface of the water around them began to churn beyond the normal swells. A swell lifted the *Excelsior* but did not recede and lower it back down. It continued to rise until the deck towered above the tallest of the oceanic mounds.

Captain Farthing shuffled to the rail, grabbed hold, and gazed over the side. "Surely they cannot be returning."

"Certainly not the ship!" Captain Lancette said. "Amelia cracked her in two."

Amelia shook her head. "No. This is bigger. Much bigger."

Captain Farthing snapped his head around. "What could be bigger than that monstrosity of a ship?"

Massive tentacles shot from the sea like missiles, each as big around as the *Excelsior's* main mast.

"Romut," Amelia said in little more than a whisper.

Captain Lancette gripped his sword in a trembling hand and gasped out, "How in the holy hells do we fight that?"

"You don't," Amelia said then shouted, "Get everyone below decks. This is no battle for mortals."

"Kraken!" Captain Farthing screamed as loud as he could and began barking orders. "Get your backsides below decks, you scallywags! We have no part to play in a battle between saints and evil gods."

The crew grabbed their fallen and hastened for the nearest deck hatch to ride out the second wave of the battle knowing their support lie not in swinging weapons but deep in prayer.

Amelia slashed at a questing tentacle when it came near. The massive appendage swiftly retreated when she struck it, scoring a deep wound that hissed and burned from her glowing holy weapon.

"You'll have to do better than that, you wish.com anime kaiju butthole!" She roared in defiance.

Romut replied to her attack and insult by striking at her from three sides at once. Its massive tentacles slammed against the deck, cracking the planking, toppling a mast, and sweeping a large swath of crates, bodies, and anything not firmly attached to the ship into the ocean.

Amelia knew she could not remain on the ship or Romut would surely rip it apart, dooming all souls aboard, trying to get to her. Angel wings made of golden light sprang from her back and she leapt into the air. Amelia beat her luminous wings and weaved between Romut's flailing appendages like a pilot in a dogfight trying to shake off enemy pursuers.

She slashed at any tentacle that got within range and fired arrows of light from her conjured bow at those beyond the reach of her sword. While her arrows and slashes left obvious wounds, the creature was colossal, and even the most severe injuries healed almost before she could land another strike.

Amelia knew she needed to deliver a decisive blow. Romut was not a creature she could kill with death by a thousand papercuts. She needed death by a thousand-ton bomb.

The warrior princess narrowly dodged a tree-sized tentacle and soared skyward like a golden rocket, piercing the grey clouds until the sun shone upon her once more. She raised her sword high over her head (resisting the urge to shout *Thundercats, ho!*) and began drawing in the power of light to vanquish the oppressive shadow of doom.

Amelia glowed like the saint she was, covered head to toe in a nimbus of golden light so bright she became a second sun. She dove back through the clouds, her sword leading as she shouted, "Super Saiyan Meteor Smash!"

The clouds parted and burned away as Amelia tore through them. Her brilliant form lit up the sky and shattered the oppressive gloom.

She impacted the water at fantastic speed, but not before one of Romut's massive tentacles swatted her like a fly.

Amelia barely registered the volcanic eruption of water created by the impact of both body and tentacle. All sound became muted as she plunged deep into the ocean depths and darkness overcame her.

With the barest remaining sliver of consciousness, Amelia felt a hand grasp hold of her and lift her back to the surface.

The unexpected knock at the door caused a bit of coffee to splash over the rim of Amelia's mother's cup. She snapped her head toward the door as her husband stood up from the small kitchenette table.

"Who could that be?" Dan asked as he strode toward the door.

"No one with good news, I'm sure," Linda said with a nervous shake of her head.

Dan opened the door to find a hotel staff member standing behind a soaking wet Amelia.

Amelia slapped her sodden wig into her father's hands as she stalked past him toward the bathroom. "Here ya go, Dad. Got ma crown wet."

Amelia's mother stood. "Amelia, how did you get all wet?

"Fighting pirates!" Amelia replied.

"I told you not to go out in the rain!"

"I wasn't in the rain," Amelia said.

The young man from the hotel cleared his throat. "Amelia...uh, had a little incident in the lobby fountain."

"What on earth possessed you to play in the fountain?" Linda snapped.

"Because pirates are found on the water. Duh," Amelia explained, her voice echoing from the bathroom. "The only place you find pirates on land is a tavern, and you have to be twenty-one to go in there. Besides, I think you'd agree, a tavern is no place for a young lady. Even a warrior queen."

"Thank you, we're very sorry for the disruption," Dan said. "She can get a bit carried away with her antics."

The young man smiled back. "It's no problem, Mr. Poole. She put on quite a show for all the guests in the lobby. We just didn't want her to catch cold or anything."

"Thank you for bringing her back. We'll make sure it doesn't happen again."

Dan closed the door, sat back at the table, and began sipping his coffee once more.

Linda shook her head as she looked toward the bathroom. "What are we going to do with that girl?"

Dan smiled over the rim of his cup. "Love her like there is no tomorrow."

CHAPTER 7

Amelia woke to the sound of her father shouting at someone. The fact she was unable to hear the other person made her think he must be on the phone. This level of hostility was usually reserved for the insurance company.

She rubbed the sleep from her eyes and shuffled from her room. Adventuring was exhausting, and it was taking its toll on her. Whenever she was not at the clinic getting subjected to a battery of tests, needle pricks, and blood draining, she had Otis take her to a new world desperate for the freedom and safety only Amelia the warrior queen could provide. At least, when she was not too tired and sick to go.

"What do you mean I need to submit forms?" her father snapped. "Dr. Fowler already sent you people a letter detailing why we need this treatment! Well, every minute I am on the phone arguing with you is a minute a sick little girl isn't getting the treatment she needs. Yeah, you do that!" Dan mashed his thumb against the screen to end the call. "Damn bureaucratic bullcrap!"

"What's wrong, Daddy?"

Dan looked over at his daughter and all the anger fled from his body. "Just dealing with some paperwork problems. So, what's on the warrior queen's agenda for today?"

"I'm just a princess. I decided I like being a princess better."

"What's wrong with being a queen?"

Amelia pressed her lips together and frowned. "Too much bureaucratic bullcrap."

"Amelia!" her mom snapped over the sound of her dad's laughter.

"I'm going to go play."

Linda stood with her fist pressed against her hip. "You're going to eat breakfast."

Amelia sat at the small dinette table. "Fine. I'll have Cocoa Puffs."

"You'll have Cheerios. You don't need all that sugar."

Amelia made a face. "Bleh, Cheerios are Fruit Loops for old people."

Her dad looked over the top of the newspaper he was reading. "Hey, I like Cheerios."

Amelia raised an empty glass and banged it against the table. "Your Honor, the defense rests its case."

"The judge bangs the gavel, not the lawyers, sweetheart," her dad said.

"It's my trial and I decide who bangs what."

Her mom plunked a bowl of Cheerios in front of her. "Breakfast is not a trial."

"It is when you might barf at any given second. Oh no, I think I feel one coming on now." Amelia pulled a party popper she had bought in the hotel gift shop out of a pocket, held it under her chin, and dry-heaved. She yanked the string and launched tiny paper streamers over the top of her dad's newspaper and onto his head and glasses. "Oh no, it's everywhere, and it smells like Cheerios!"

Her mom huffed out a loud breath. "It does not."

Amelia pulled a soggy, errant streamer out of her cereal bowl. "This one does."

"Eat," her mom ordered.

She dug into her cereal with faked enthusiasm until there was nothing but a small puddle of milk and tan specks left in the bottom of the bowl. "Can I go play now?"

Her mom looked as if she wanted to object but she sighed and nodded her head. "Make sure you take my phone, and try not to bother anyone."

Amelia jammed the cell phone in her pocket and ran to the door. "Later, taters!"

"And stay out of the water!" her mother shouted after her.

She sprinted down the hall, weaved around a cleaning cart, and turned sideways to squeeze through the elevator doors before they completely opened. She found Otis sitting on a stool in the corner taking a pair of scissors to a newspaper.

"Whatcha doing, clipping coupons?"

Otis smiled up at her and shook his head. "Reviews."

"Movie reviews?"

"Play reviews."

"Why?" Amelia asked.

"I have a friend who writes plays, and she doesn't like to read the reviews, Otis replied"

"Are they that bad?"

"Oh no, they are almost always praising, but she says her plays are for the people, not for her, and especially not for the critics."

"That's nice of you to do that for her," Amelia said with a nod.

"She's a very special friend," Otis replied said with a sparkle in his eyes that hinted they were much more than friends.

"What's her name?"

"Lilith."

Amelia gave Otis an impish grin. "Do you love her?"

Otis chuckled. "I suppose I do."

"Does she love you?"

"I suppose she does."

"Then why aren't you married? You aren't married, are you?"

Otis smiled at an ancient memory and shook his head. "No, we aren't married."

"Why not? If you love each other, then you should get married."

"It's complicated."

"What's so complicated about love? You love each other, you get married, and you have wonderful children like me—if you're really lucky. If not, then you get a turd like Bradley."

Otis set the scissors on his lap and laughed. Amelia loved his laugh. It was deep, sonorous, and authentic.

"We have loved each other for a very long time, and people like her did not associate with, much less marry, people like me back then. We were lucky she inherited the hotel after her father passed away. She was able to keep me on as an elevator operator long after modern technology made me obsolete, just so we could be close."

Amelia crossed her arms and scowled. "That's stupid. People should marry who they want. Who cares what they do for a living?"

"Like I said, it was complicated."

"I guess you have to be a grown-up to be confused, because it seems pretty simple to me."

Otis nodded and folded the newspaper. "You have the right of it. So, where to today?"

Amelia chewed her lip as she thought. "I'm not sure. I've been just about everywhere I want to go. What do you think?"

"Well, maybe it's not about where you want to go but where you're most needed."

Amelia slapped her palm against her forehead. "Duh, I must be becoming an adult. It's so obvious. Otis, take me to where I am most needed."

Otis pressed a button on the console. "Very good, Miss Amelia."

Amelia could never tell if the elevator was traveling up or down. Often, it felt like it was moving in both directions at once and sometimes even sideways. However, the ride did seem to take longer this time.

When the doors slid open, Amelia could only stare. She had been shocked to step out of an elevator onto the deck of a sailing ship, but what she saw before her was especially mind-blowing.

Through the rectangular opening was a verdant jungle the likes of which she had never imagined. Massive trees soared overhead while broad-leaved plants and bushes with enormous, fragrant flowers covered the ground. A waterfall cascaded over a cliff in the distance, and a stream gurgled not far outside of the elevator doors and coursed across the ground to join the larger river below the falls.

Amelia looked at Otis. "What am I supposed to do?"

Otis smiled down at her. "Sorry, kid, I'm no spoiler. You must figure that out for yourself."

The warrior princess gnawed her bottom lip and stepped out into the jungle. She knew this was different than her previous adventures, but how so she could not say. The air was cooler than she had expected, not balmy like the jungles on television, and there was something electric in the atmosphere.

Amelia looked behind her, but the elevator doors closed and disappeared, leaving only the unblemished backdrop of the jungle. She had started walking toward the stream when a loud strumming sound caught her attention. The noise reminded her of the time a hornet buzzed by her ear and stung her on the shoulder. Hornets were jerks, and these ones, she was sure it was more than one, sounded a *lot* bigger.

She took cover behind a leaf the size of a beach towel and conjured her silver armor, shield, and weaponry. If that hornet thought to abuse her, it was in for a nasty surprise, no matter how big it was.

CHAPTER 8

As the droning drew near, Amelia was able to distinguish the sound of two separate creatures, and if the shadows they cast on the ground were anywhere true to their size, they were nearly as big as she was. Leaves and sticks crunched underfoot not far away and the buzzing stopped.

"Hey, whatch'a doing back there?" a high-pitched, girlish voice asked.

"Leave her alone," a boy replied. "She might be going pee."

"Please, warrior princesses do not go pee."

"Of course they do! Otherwise, they would blow up like a water balloon until they popped."

Amelia peered out from behind the leaf and saw a boy and a girl her age dressed in colorful silk clothes. Both were as bald as she was but had elaborate blue markings scrawled all over their heads. The strangest thing by far was the double pair of gossamer wings sprouting from their backs, like those of a dragonfly.

She stood up and took a step toward the pair. "I wasn't going pee. I thought you were giant hornets."

The girl shrieked and clapped her hands. "It *is* you! I knew you would come! See, Felix, I told you if we danced hard enough, they would send a warrior princess to save us!"

"Save you from what? How do you know I'm a warrior princess?"

The boy, Felix, said, "The whole village has been performing the dance of deliverance for days in hopes of summoning someone to help us destroy the demons and the Blight. As for knowing who you are, your sword and staff show you are a warrior, and your tribal markings indicate you are of a royal family."

"Tribal markings?" Amelia wondered aloud, kneeling next to the stream, and gazing at her reflection.

She gasped when she saw the designs decorating her bald scalp. They were twice as numerous and complex as those of the boy and the girl. Amelia dipped her hand in the water and ran it over her head. As she suspected, she was unable to even smudge the lines. Her mother was going to freak out when she saw them.

Amelia stood up and turned back to the pair. "Who are you?"

"I'm Ophelia and that's my brother Felix," the girl said.

"My name is Amelia."

Amelia tried not to look at their wings. Her mother always said it was rude to stare at people because they were different, something she fully appreciated these days. The siblings beat their wings and lifted a few feet off the ground.

Ophelia beckoned to her and said, "Come on, Amelia, everyone is going to love to meet you!"

"Uh, okay, but try to keep it slow. I don't have wings like you two."

Felix and Ophelia gave each other confused smiles and Ophelia said, "Of course you do, silly. All of us fairies have wings."

Amelia looked over her shoulder "But I'm not a...fairy..."

Her armor now had two slots in the back and through them sprouted a double pair of glossy wings.

"Okay, so I have wings. That's new," she whispered to herself. "How the heck do I make them work?"

Amelia's wings beat an insane staccato the moment she formed the thought. The sudden lift sent her windmilling, her toes barely touching the ground. Her feet settled back to earth, or wherever the heck she was, and her wings quieted the instant she willed them to stop.

"Are you okay, Amelia?" Ophelia asked.

Amelia felt her face flush. "Yeah, I'm fine. It was just a long trip, and I'm a little tired, is all. I think I'm okay now. Lead the way."

The fairy siblings lit into the air once again and Amelia followed. Flying was not as difficult as she had first feared. In fact, it was quite easy, and it was not as if she were a complete novice at it.

Amelia performed several barrel rolls and flew loops around Ophelia and Felix in a corkscrew pattern, laughing and whooping with joy all the while. Their flight turned into a game of catch me if you can with Ophelia in the lead, followed by her brother, and then the newcomer.

Not knowing where they were going, Amelia stuck close behind Felix while gawking at the amazing panoramic beauty all around her. The jungle was lush and green with enormous, colorful flowers dotting the emerald landscape. Cliffs of grey and black stone jutted up out of the forest canopy over which waterfalls cascaded down through the trees and into rivers below.

Ophelia rocketed up one of the cliff faces and vanished over the precipice. Amelia chased after her, feeling the water spray misting over her exposed skin and beading up on her armor. She zipped over the edge after Felix and nearly collided with them both as they hovered in the air just beyond the rim.

"Hey, what do you…?" Amelia began to protest, but she cut off her words as she gazed out toward the horizon.

The verdant jungle gave way to black ruin for as far as the eye could see. No birds flew, no flowers grew, and the trees were twisted, decaying monstrosities.

"What happened?" Amelia asked in a quiet voice.

"It's the Blight," Felix answered. "It's why we summoned you."

"What am I supposed to do? How do I fix this?"

Ophelia said, "You must kill the demon who caused this. He summons minions to spread his disease across the land. No matter how many we defeat, he just creates more. We have tried to stop them, but they are too many, and we aren't strong enough to kill their master. That's why we need you."

"What's his name?" Amelia asked, even as her stomach churned, knowing without a doubt who was responsible.

"Romut," Felix said, his voice tight with anger and fear.

"I figured as much."

"You know him?" Ophelia asked.

"He's been my nemesis for as long as I can remember. He's gone too far this time. I won't let him escape again."

Ophelia looked at Amelia with hopeful eyes. "You can defeat him?"

Amelia smiled. "Are you kidding? I've kicked his butt a hundred times. This won't be any different. Don't worry, you have a warrior princess on your side."

Ophelia spun a half-circle. "Come on, let's get to the village. We can talk about the Blight later. It's time to party!"

The fairy twins hurled themselves over the waterfall's edge and raced toward the jungle canopy. They skimmed over the treetops at breakneck speeds, the foliage a green blur beneath them. Colorful birds flew up and joined their little aerial squadron for a few brief moments before giving up the playful chase and disappearing back into the forest.

Ophelia and Felix made an unexpected dive into the treetops. Amelia hastily corrected her flight and caught several leaves in her face as she followed them down. She burst through the lower canopy and nearly collided with Felix as he hovered next to his sister.

"Hey, you wanna put some brake lights on your butt or something?" Amelia said as her wings beat an angry buzz to arrest her flight.

Felix grinned and stuck his tongue out at her.

"Welcome to Ardentia," Ophelia said with a grand wave of her hand.

Amelia gazed into the trees before her, and her eyes widened in wonderment.

"Whoa," she responded in a long breath.

The village, or city to Amelia's eyes, spread through the jungle before her. The homes and other buildings were grown, not constructed, within the verdant boughs. Supple limbs were woven together to create walls, floors, and roofs without harming the trees from which they were created.

Light shimmered throughout the village, glittering off crystals and polished bits of metal hanging from almost every branch like ornaments on a Christmas tree. And there were fairies everywhere. They zipped and buzzed through the trees and between homes in a carefree, aerial dance that took them on winding, circuitous routes to their destinations.

Ophelia nudged Amelia's shoulder. "Come on, you have to meet Maala."

The warrior princess followed her down into the village. "Who's Maala?"

"She's our leader," Ophelia called over her shoulder.

They landed on a balcony of braided vines. The home was a little bigger and slightly more elaborate than those around it but certainly nothing that would distinguish it as a royal residence. It was a rather modest home for a queen.

A fairy dressed in shimmering silk, her feet bare like everyone else, strode out onto the balcony a moment after their arrival. She was beautiful, just like every other fairy Amelia had seen, but Maala was the only one she had noticed thus far who appeared to have aged fully into adulthood. She looked like the mother of these thousands of young people.

Amelia bowed. "Um…Your Highness. Sorry, I'm not sure of your title."

Maala smiled, creating a few tiny creases next to her lips and in the corners of her eyes. "We do not stand on formality here. Just call me Maala, or Mother, as you please. You must be Princess Amelia."

"I am. Ophelia and Felix showed me the Blight. I'm so sorry. I'll do whatever I can to help."

"We are all grateful for your arrival. We were not sure if you would hear our song, but Felix and Ophelia believed strongly enough for us all, and so here you are."

"How long has Romut been plaguing this land?" Amelia asked.

Maala's face fell. "The Blight started quite some time ago. For years, we were able to combat it. We could not force it to retreat, but we did slow its advance—until recently. Romut had left the Blight to his demons while he went and did whatever it is evil does. But now that he has returned and taken a direct hand in the destruction, it has spread far and wide. Many of the people you see here are refugees from villages already lost to the Blight. It will not be long before it consumes Ardentia, and if Ardentia falls, there is little to stop it from destroying the whole world."

Tears welled up in Amelia's eyes just thinking about the death of this beautiful jungle and its inhabitants. "I won't let that happen. I have beaten Romut before, and I'll do it again."

Maala smiled. "With your help, I am certain we will win, but first, we must celebrate your arrival."

CHAPTER 9

Maala hovered in the center of a clearing surrounded by her people. "Fairies of Ardentia and welcome guests, long have we danced and sent our song of salvation out into the world. Today, I am happy to announce that our plea has been heard. Amelia, the warrior princess herself, has come to our aid. With her strength, we shall destroy the Blight and banish the evil Romut from our world forever!"

The people cheered so loud that the crystals and chimes hanging from the trees vibrated with a clear resonance like a string struck by a piano's hammer, the note held long after the impact.

"Let us show our appreciation the fairy way—in dance!" Maala declared.

Ophelia squeezed Amelia's hand. "You're going to love this. This is how we called to you."

Amelia tried to ask what she meant, but she and Felix flitted into the crowd. The wings of a thousand fairies began to beat, and the crystals took up a harmony, keeping perfect time with the people's strumming wingbeats and rhythmic dancing. The congregation began to circle until Amelia felt as if she were standing in the eye of a tornado.

The fairies danced around her in what appeared to be a waltz, and the crystals made music as clear and sonorous as an orchestra, mimicking the sounds of every instrument Amelia had ever heard and many that were alien yet beautiful to her ears. The dance went on, culminating several minutes later as an amazing ballet of twirls and aerial leaps.

Maala and the twins rejoined Amelia in the center of the clearing when the music and dancing finally came to an end.

"What did you think?" Felix asked.

Amelia grinned brightly. "It was amazing! The way everyone danced and how the crystals made music was incredible. I've never seen anything like it."

Maala beamed and shifted her gaze outward to the fairies surrounding them and said in a loud voice, "Perhaps Princess Amelia will grace us with a dance of her people?"

The crowd cheered and applauded. Amelia's grin vanished and her face flushed.

"I don't know anything about dancing or making music!" she whispered.

"Don't worry," Ophelia replied, "it's just like flying. All you must do is think about what you want. The crystals will make the music for you and your wings will help you dance."

"I don't know..." Amelia said, but the expectant looks she got from everyone nudged her forward.

Amelia was never much into music, but there was one song they played in the cancer ward at least four or five times a day, so she knew it by heart. She hoped they would like it. It was very different from the fairies' more formal style of music and dance.

With a resigned sigh, Amelia started playing the song in her head. She flew in time with the music that the crystals made by translating her thoughts and wingbeats into sound. The tune was a little shaky at first and her dance a bit stilted and unsure, but Amelia closed her eyes, gave herself over to the music, and danced like no one was watching. In moments, Rachel Platten's "Fight Song" filled the jungle.

Amelia launched into a chaotic routine of flips and aerial acrobatics that looked more like a performance by the Blue Angels at an airshow than a dance. Her sword was in her hand, cutting bright streaks of light with every swing and twirl as she rhythmically cavorted through an invisible horde of demons.

She finished the dance with her sword held over her head in both hands, the blade shining like a star. Amelia fought to catch her breath as she looked out at the crowd expectantly.

Silence greeted her as everyone stared, eyes wide and mouths agape.

Amelia's face burned red. "Uh...sorry. I guess I got a little carried away."

The sudden roar and applause were deafening. Everyone cheered so loud Amelia was afraid the crystals would shatter or get blown from the trees. Ophelia and Felix rushed to her side.

"That was the most amazing thing I have ever seen!" Ophelia exclaimed. "You have to teach me your music!"

"Me too!" Felix chimed in.

"Uh, yeah, sure, if I can. I'm not even sure how I did it though."

Amelia noticed an insistent buzzing coming from her pocket. She pulled out her phone and read the text on the screen. "Aw crap."

"What is that?" Ophelia asked.

"It's called a phone," Amelia answered. "It's a device moms use to wreck your fun. I have to go home, but I'll come back as soon as I can."

Maala swooped in and hugged her. "I will rally our people for battle and await your return."

"I'll be back soon, I promise."

Amelia saw that she had missed several demands to come home for lunch and beat her wings with all haste to take her back to the elevator—only she was not sure where exactly it was. The jungle was vast and one part looked like any other. She had barely formed the worrying thought in her mind when the elevator appeared, the doors sliding open to reveal Otis' smiling face.

"How was it?" he asked.

"It was awesome! I met the fairies and they danced, and then I danced all crazy-like but they loved it and cheered!" Amelia's face took on a sour look. "Romut is here, and he is killing the forest. I have to come back and kick his butt, but Mom says I need to come home for lunch first."

"Well, then we best get you back to the hotel."

The doors swished shut and the elevator went into motion. It stopped a minute later and deposited her onto her room's floor. Amelia waved to Otis as she scampered down the hall. Using her plastic keycard to open the door, she burst into the room. The expression on her mother's face quelled her excitement.

"Where have you been?" her mom demanded. "I have been texting and calling you for the last twenty minutes. I was almost ready to call the police!"

Amelia screwed up her face. "Erm…I guess the jungle has spotty cell reception."

"What jungle?" Linda stopped and stared at her daughter. "What is all over your head?"

"They're my tribal markings. Aren't they cool?" Amelia asked, her voice rising to a near shout.

"Very cool, dear," her dad replied.

"They are not cool! You look ridiculous." Her mom stormed over, licked her thumb, and began vigorously rubbing at one of the designs. "Is this permanent marker? It is going to take forever to get these off."

"I don't want them off. They're better than hair. It marks me as a warrior princess."

"It marks you as a child with poor supervision," her mom said.

"It's my head. Dad, can I get them tattooed on?"

Dan opened his mouth but Linda cut him off. "Of course you cannot get them tattooed!"

Amelia stuck out her chin and stamped her foot. "Why not?"

Linda stared wide-eyed and leaned forward as if she were answering the dumbest question ever asked. "Because tattoos last your whole life."

Amelia crossed her arms and pouted. "So, these probably will too."

Linda's mouth dropped open and her eyes boiled over with tears. "Go to your room," she choked out.

"I don't have a room," Amelia snapped back. "I have a couch. Do you want me to go to my couch?"

"Go to my room!"

Amelia stomped her foot. "Fine!"

Linda kept her composure until her daughter slammed the bedroom door before she broke down and sobbed into her hands. Dan rushed to her side and held her before she collapsed to the floor.

"I'm sorry," Linda said, wiping her hands across her eyes. "I'm not even mad at her or her silly drawings. I just can't accept all of this. It's not fair!"

"I know. Do you think I am having an easier time with it? I'm just a better actor than you are. Inside, I am raging and screaming and crying. I am throwing an epic tantrum and giving God the finger with both hands."

"How do you do it?" Linda asked with a loud sniff.

"I do it for her. It is the only thing I can do for her now."

Linda sighed and stood up straight. "You're right. I need to keep it together for her." She crossed the living room and knocked on the door before opening it. "Amelia, honey."

Amelia looked up from where she was sitting on the bed, blood marring her nose and spotting the pillow. "Mom, I'm sorry I got blood on the pillow. It was an accident."

Linda rushed to the bathroom connected to the bedroom and came out with a damp rag. "Dan!" she shouted as she wiped the blood from Amelia's face.

Dan burst into the room. "What? What's wrong?"

"We need to get to the hospital, now!"

Amelia looked up at her mother. "It's okay. It's just a bloody nose."

Linda rubbed at one of Amelia's markings and forced a smile. "Of course it is, but we still need to have the doctor take a look at it."

Amelia's tiny shoulders slumped. "Ugh, I hate going to the hospital. It's so boring, and it smells funny."

"We still need to go. Let's get your coat."

CHAPTER 10

Amelia suffered through yet another session inside the clunking coffin that was the MRI machine before being wheeled to a private room and forced into bed.

"Please tell me I don't have to stay here," Amelia said.

"We have to wait for the doctor to take a look at your pictures," Linda replied.

Amelia crossed her arms and sulked. "This must be how the people at Guantanamo feel."

Her father chuckled. "This is not a prison and you are not a terrorist."

"Allyoucaneat snackbar!" she shouted, then gave a throaty laugh.

Linda sat in a chair next to her bed and stroked her daughter's head.

Amelia rolled her eyes up in their sockets toward her mother's hand. "Mom, I'm sorry I drew on my head."

Linda smiled down at her. "It's all right, sweetie. I wasn't really mad about that. I'm just sad that you are sick. I really don't care what you draw on yourself. If it makes you happy, go ahead and do it."

"Can I tattoo my head then?" she asked with a mischievous grin.

"When you turn eighteen, you can tattoo whatever you want. But no tramp stamps!"

Amelia screwed her face up. "What's a tramp stamp?"

Dan leaned down on the other side of her bed. "It's what mommies get in college then pay someone a lot of money to remove after they find out they are pregnant."

"Dan!" Linda cried.

"Mom, you had a tattoo?" Amelia asked, wide-eyed. "Where was it?"

Linda's face flushed. "It's none of your business."

"I want to see a picture! Dad, do you have any pictures?"

"Dan, don't you dare," Linda ordered before he could answer.

Dr. Fowler arrived and saved Linda from further inquiry and embarrassment. "Dan, Linda, would you like to follow me to my office."

Linda kissed Amelia's head and stood up. "Sit tight. We'll be right back."

"Can I have your phone? I want to play Angry Birds."

She reached into her purse and handed over the device. "Only if you promise to behave yourself."

"I always behave myself," the girl responded, insulted by the insinuation.

"Behave like a fool maybe," her dad chimed in.

Amelia responded by sticking her tongue out at him.

Dan and Linda followed the doctor to her office with leaden steps, their worst fears playing out in their minds. They took a seat and held hands so tightly it was uncomfortable, but the fear of the doctor's impending diagnosis overwhelmed all tactile sensation.

"What's the news, doctor?" Dan managed to ask.

Dr. Fowler sighed. "Not good, I'm afraid."

The strength of Linda's grip redoubled.

Dr. Fowler displayed the MRI images on a large screen attached to the wall. "The mass has increased by a surprising amount and is now putting excessive pressure on the surrounding regions of the brain."

"What does this mean for her?" Linda asked in a quavering voice.

"It means that none of the noninvasive treatments are working anymore, and surgery is now our only option."

"But you said surgery was dangerous."

The doctor nodded. "It is, but it is now less dangerous than attempting any other form of treatment available to us."

Dan fought to swallow the lump in his throat so he could speak. "When do you want to do it?"

"As soon as possible. I have tentatively scheduled the operating room for her on Friday."

"Five days," Dan whispered. "What is her prognosis, really?"

Dr. Fowler's shoulders slumped and she frowned. "It isn't good. If you have any family who wants to see her, you should make arrangements before the surgery."

Dan felt his wife trembling as she took several deep breaths.

Linda steeled her resolve and directed a grim smile at her husband. "I can do this—for her."

There was a slight hesitation in Dr. Fowler's voice as she intruded on the parents' emotional turmoil. "Do you want me to go ahead and secure the O.R. for her surgery?"

Dan nodded and barely managed to croak out, "Yes."

It was a sullen and somber trudge back to Amelia's room. Amelia, true to form, shattered the seriousness of the moment the instant her parents walked in.

"Mom, you had a tattoo on your butt crack?" she crowed, holding up the cell phone with the image of a woman's tattoo.

Linda shrugged the weight of her sorrow from her shoulders. "It was my lower back, not my butt crack."

Dan chortled. "Yeah, very lower back," and received a sharp jab in the ribs from his wife's elbow.

"You were supposed to be playing Angry Birds, not looking up tattoos on the Internet," Linda said.

Amelia swiped her finger across the screen a few times and held up a picture of a tattoo of Tweety Bird smoking a cigarette and flipping everyone off emblazoned just above a woman's backside. "This one looks pretty angry."

Linda reached down and snatched the phone from Amelia's hand. "You can watch TV."

"Aw man, TV is so boring."

"We'll be back in a couple of hours," her dad promised.

"You're leaving me here?"

"Sorry, kiddo, doctor's orders. Your mom and I need to go make some phone calls, so why don't you take a nap? We'll be back when you wake up," Dan replied.

"I can't stay here! I have to go help the fairies fight Romut."

"Romut will have to wait."

"Evil waits for no man…or warrior princess."

Linda kissed her forehead. "You are very sick. The doctors are going to try something in a few days. After that, then you can go fight the fairies."

"I'm not fighting the fairies, Mom! I'm fighting *with* the fairies against Romut. Duh!"

"Don't duh me, and everyone will just have to play nice until you get better."

"Fine. Later taters!"

Linda managed to maintain her composure until the elevator doors closed. She was grateful for the handrail as it was the only thing holding her up.

CHAPTER II

"Oh my God, this is so boring!" Amelia complained for the umpteenth time.

"What are you talking about?" Tyler asked. "This is *Lord of the Rings*. How is it boring?"

"Seen it, lived it, bored of it." She looked around the TV room full of children much like herself and sighed. "There has to be something else to do in this place."

"Aren't your parents coming soon?" Jordan asked. She was one of the lucky few who still had hair. It was dark and curly, and while Amelia loved her warrior sigils, she relished the idea of having a warm head without needing to wear a hat.

"Oh yeah, they're a real ray of sunshine. You think cancer is depressing? Try being around my mom for five minutes."

Tyler leaned over in his chair and whispered, "I hear they have a swimming pool downstairs."

"No way!" Amelia hissed back. "Why would a hospital have a swimming pool?"

"Physical therapy for people who have trouble walking and stuff," Tyler replied.

"I haven't been swimming in forever," Amelia said.

"Me either," Jordan said.

"We have to go check it out," Amelia said in a whisper.

"There's no way they will let us go to the pool," Tyler countered.

A mischievous grin spread across Amelia's face. "Who said anything about getting permission?"

Jordan's smile mirrored Amelia's. "Are you talking about a jailbreak?"

Amelia nodded. "I'm talking about a jailbreak."

Tyler interjected as the voice of dissent. "Guys, we could get in a lot of trouble for leaving the ward, not to mention invading the swimming pool."

"We have freaking cancer," Amelia snapped. "Who gives a baboon's red butt about getting in trouble?"

"She has a point," Jordan said.

Tyler rolled his eyes. "This is why girls should get more spankings. You are all crazy."

Amelia smiled. "Being a princess has its perks. So, are you in or out?"

Tyler shrugged. "Like you said, I have cancer. What are they going to do to me? I'm in."

All three children leaned in close together and Amelia said, "Okay, I'll work on the distraction. You two go around and find out who's with us and get them close to the doors without drawing any attention to yourselves."

"When do we make our move?" Jordan asked.

"You'll know when. Just have everyone follow me," Amelia replied.

The group split up with Tyler and Jordon seeking out allies. Amelia identified the sickest kids in the room, those who were restricted to wheelchairs or confined to their beds but were still rolled into the recreation room for some socialization. She sidled up to one of the beds and leaned on the rail.

"Hey, Michael."

Michael turned his head and looked at Amelia with hollowed eyes. "Hey, Amelia. I like your designs."

She absently touched her head. "Thanks."

"I hear you're going under the knife tomorrow. They'll have to scrub them all off."

"Yeah. Mom says I can't get them tattooed on until I'm eighteen."

Michael blew a raspberry. "Moms…"

"I know, right? Anyway, me and some of the other kids are going to make a break for it, but we need your help."

Michael gave her a sidelong glance. "What are you up to?"

"We're going to raid the swimming pool downstairs."

"Nice!" Michael replied with a soft laugh. "What do you need from me?"

"When I give you the signal, I need you to pull the plug and set off the alarms."

"Ah, so I'm the distraction."

Amelia nodded. "We can't do it without you. You are a crucial element to our plan."

"Like Ocean's—" Michael made a quick count of the children in the room "—Fifteen."

"Exactly. Can you do it?"

"Sure can."

"Awesome. Maybe throw in a little glitch and twitch to really get the nurses stirred up."

Michael grinned and flashed her a thumbs-up. Amelia made a circuit around the room, enlisting others and laying out her plans. Once complete, she met up with Jordan and Tyler near the ward's entrance.

"Is this everyone who's going?" Amelia asked as she looked around at the faces hovering over a Monopoly board.

Jordan nodded. "Yep. We have seven runners, counting us. Did you get our distraction set up?"

"Done. Is everyone ready to bolt?"

The faces around the table all nodded, some of the kids bouncing up and down in their excitement to do something other than stand or lie around praying to get better. Amelia caught Michael's eyes and nodded.

Michael cleared his throat to signal the other distractors before moving the pulse oximeter clip from his finger to one he had wrapped a Band-Aid around so as to foul its sensor. An alarm wailed at the sudden loss of a heartbeat and lack of detectable oxygen in the blood. More audible warnings rang out as some of the other kids performed similar acts of sabotage.

Nurses burst through the door in seconds and hustled through the ward. Amelia and the other runners darted for the door and caught it before it clicked shut and locked them inside. It took only moments for the nurses to realize the charade.

"Hey, you kids get back here!" Amelia heard Nurse Lisa shout through the slowly closing door.

Nurse Lisa moved to chase after the fleeing children but found her way blocked by several kids in wheelchairs. Amelia whooped as she saw her plan unfolding exactly how she had hoped.

"Which way to the stairs?" Tyler asked as they slid to a stop at the hall's intersection.

Jordan saw the sign indicating that the stairs were to their left. "That way!"

Slippered feet slapped against the linoleum floor as the children raced down the hallway, some of them pushing IV poles ahead of them, setting the liquid-filled bags swaying.

"Oh my God, I forgot how tiring running is these days," Jordan gasped, noticeably slowing along with the others.

Amelia looked back at the sound of pursuit and saw Nurse Lisa and Nurse Steve round the corner. She yanked the door open to the stairwell and ushered everyone inside. "Keep going. I'll slow them down."

She picked up a plastic pitcher of water from a nearby food cart and poured it out onto the floor in front of the door. Amelia then grabbed the fire extinguisher stored in a small recess next to the stairwell door, pulled the pin, and squeezed the handle. The extinguisher bucked but she held on tight and directed a blast at the thin pool of water.

"You shall not pass!" she cried as the CO_2 erupted from the big black nozzle in a frigid cloud and froze the puddle solid in seconds.

She set the discharged fire extinguisher down on the landing and shoved the heavy fire door shut in the nurses' faces. Nurse Steve tried to push it open but his feet slipped on the ice. His face disappeared from the small window in a flash and Amelia heard him hit the floor with a loud curse. She wedged the pitcher handle under the door and ran after her friends. Jordan waited two floors down and beckoned for her to follow.

The slower kids were just ahead as Amelia, Tyler, and Jordan caught up with them. They followed the signs giving directions to the physical therapy pool and burst into the enormous room with raucous whoops of joy and shrill cheers. Those not tethered to IV poles leapt into the shallow end of the pool while the constrained children sat on the edge and kicked their feet in the water.

"Hey, what are you kids doing down here?" one of the physical therapists called out.

The patients using the pool just watched and smiled, some laughing as loudly as the children who paid the grown-ups no attention. Even Nurse Steve and Nurse Lisa could not help but stand and smile when they found their wayward charges moments later. Amelia caught Nurse Linda's mock glare and waved. The nurse's bemused look slid from her face and a look of real concern replaced it.

The sudden change confused Amelia until her vision began to swim and her legs turned rubbery. She looked down at the crimson ring spreading out around her, and her heart leapt.

Amelia wiped her nose and stared at the blood covering her hand. "Aw crap," she muttered before her legs gave out and she slipped under the water.

She felt herself floating even after she knew someone had carried her out of the pool and laid her on the floor.

"We've got a code blue in the therapy pool!" someone shouted.

The words were echoey in Amelia's ears, as if she were still underwater. A bright light flashed in her left eye and then her right.

"Amelia? Amelia, can you hear me, sweetheart?"

Amelia tried to answer Nurse Linda. Her lips moved but she was unable to form words. Other people arrived and someone lifted her onto a gurney. Overhead lights flashed by as she was raced down the hall. She closed her eyes and let the darkness take her away from the chaos.

CHAPTER 12

"Amelia. Amelia, you have to wake up. We need your help." Amelia looked around but saw only darkness. "Ophelia, is that you?"

"Please, Amelia, you have to wake up before it's too late."

Amelia forced her eyes open and blinked at the sudden influx of light. She turned her head to look around and found she was in her hospital room. A machine rhythmically beeped not far away from her bedside. She bolted upright as the memory of Ophelia's plea replayed itself in her mind. The fairies needed her.

Alarms blared when Amelia disconnected herself from the monitors and ran from her room. Someone shouted as she made her escape, but she ignored them. Amelia did not know how she was going to get all the way to the hotel, but she had to try. Her face lit up with a huge smile when the elevator doors opened and she saw Otis standing there in his uniform with a big grin on his face.

"Otis, you found me! How did you get here?"

"I run a magic elevator. I am wherever I need to be."

"You have to take me back to the fairies. They need me!"

Otis pressed a button on the panel. "Of course they do. I'll have you there in a tick."

Amelia thought about how worried her parents and the people at the hospital would be at her sudden disappearance, but she had to go. She knew they had tolerated her antics a lot these last few weeks, but they would just have to forgive her this one last thing.

The smell of death and decay struck her like a physical blow the instant the doors opened. She made a visual check of her armor and weapons and found them all in their proper place. A quick test of her wings and she was ready for battle. Amelia lifted into the air and raced for Ardentia with as much speed as she could muster. She burst through the jungle canopy and her flight faltered at what she beheld. The Blight had ravaged the forest for as far as the eye could see. She hovered in mute horror above what might be the only verdant oasis left in this land.

Amelia pushed herself onward to Ardentia, praying that she was not too late to save the fairies and what was once a beautiful world. As she drew near the village, she saw that it and its people still lived, but the Blight was closing in on them fast. Only a thin swath of living, breathing forest remained between Ardentia and encroaching pestilence.

Ophelia, Felix, and Maala darted toward her as she approached the village.

"Amelia, we thought you had abandoned us!" Ophelia said, bravely trying to hide the anguish in her voice.

"I'm so sorry," Amelia said, choking on a fearful lump in her throat. "I came back as soon as I could."

Felix nudged his sister with his elbow. "See, I told you she was coming back."

Amelia turned tearful eyes to the fairy leader. "Maala, I'm so sorry. I didn't think it would spread this fast."

"You are here now. That is what is important. The fairies have gathered, and we are ready to cast this scourge from our world. Will you lead us?"

The warrior princess gave a grim smile. "You bet. Have everyone follow me in. I will find and fight Romut. I just need your people to keep his lesser minions off me."

Felix hefted the spear in his hands. "Will do."

Amelia raised her sword over her head. "Then let's do this!"

The group of fairies became a swarm as the entire village and its refugees took to the sky. The sound of their wings reminded Amelia of a squadron of old bombers or fighter planes she had seen on one of the war documentaries her dad liked to watch. It took only minutes to leave the sunny, green jungle and plunge into the grey wastes perpetually lost in a twilight gloom.

Black demons rose up out of the Blight by the thousands, intent on destroying the last vestiges of life in this world. Amelia slashed at any who dared come within her reach. The demons bled sickly yellow ichor, which sizzled and popped when spilled by the warrior princess' silver blade.

The fairy twins flew beside her, doing their best to ward off attacks so their hero could engage the Blight's architect and end his destruction once and for all.

The fairies were fierce fighters and swift fliers. What they lacked in numbers, they made up for in skill and tenacity. They slaughtered the demons in droves, but Amelia could tell their valiant efforts were not enough. There were just too many foes, and the demon horde was steadily pushing them back.

Amelia sheathed her sword and drew her bow. She loosed arrow after arrow, the silver shafts streaking through the air like tiny missiles, which sometimes struck down half a dozen demons, so thick was the air with their kind. Still, it was not enough, and Amelia knew they were destined to fail unless she could find Romut and slay him.

Amelia's voice resonated like a battle horn. "Romut, you giant butthole, come out and fight me!"

She watched a black, amorphous blob form below her and gather until it became a mountain. The mountain took on a semblance of human form with a head, shoulders, and long, black, oily arms.

Romut's voice erupted from the mountain like a volcano, spewing filth with every word. "So, you have finally come to face the real me, little princess."

"I've come to destroy you!"

"You will fail, pathetic child. My power here is absolute. None can stand against me."

Amelia smiled as she drew back her bow. "Then it's a good thing I can fly."

Her arrow flashed through the air and buried itself in Romut's cavernous eye to the fletching. The demon king roared. Bile and pestilence flew from his mouth in vomitous gushes. His minions charged at Amelia from all directions. She shouldered her bow and drew her sword once more.

"I need some help here!" Amelia cried as she scythed through the onslaught and battled her way toward Romut.

Maala and her host of fairies raced to her aid, forcing the demons away from Amelia so she could battle the true foe. Amelia dove toward the humanoid blob, her sword trailing a streamer of silver light like a comet.

She looked almost comical, like a bird attacking a mountain, but there was nothing funny about the damage she caused. Every cut of her blade left a searing, sizzling gash in Romut's black hide. The demon king cried out in pain and fury, slapping at the buzzing, stinging little insect harrying it.

Romut raised an amorphous appendage. The bulbous end split into fingers, those fingers dividing again until each digit looked to be capped by giant octopi, and swatted at the warrior princess. Amelia's blade flashed, each swing lopping off a tentacle, but no matter how much damage she inflicted or how many appendages she severed, Romut simply grew more.

Amelia shouted in triumph when her sword hacked through one of the digits and sent an entire "octopus" falling to the ground, but her victory was short-lived. A tentacle from Romut's other arm struck her hard in the back, the impact ringing like a bell against her armor. Another rope-like limb caught her in mid-tumble, wrapped around her body, and flung her through the air.

She managed to arrest her headlong flight half a mile from where she had been fighting Romut. Amelia looked around and surveyed the battlefield. What she saw was disheartening. The demons had driven the fairies back to the edge of what remained of their arboreal homeland. Even as she watched, Amelia could see the Blight chewing into the forest, devouring more of it by the minute.

Maala, flanked by the twins, flitted beside her. "We are losing ground. If you cannot defeat Romut soon, we will not last much longer."

Amelia chewed her lip and shook her head. "He's too strong here. I can't beat him. I can't do enough damage to really hurt him."

"There must be something you can do?" Ophelia said with tears running down her cheeks.

Amelia looked from Romut's colossal form to the village and the fairies still fighting all around her. One of the few remaining sunbeams still able to pierce the gloom enshrouding the land reflected off something in the village, sending out a radiant, multihued glimmer of light.

"I have it!" Amelia said. "Have everyone fall back to the village."

"We cannot fight them in our home. We will surely lose everything if we do," Maala said.

Amelia smiled. "We aren't going to fight them. We are going to destroy them."

"How?" Felix asked.

"By dancing."

Maala's eyes glittered as she came to understand what Amelia wanted to do. She raised a horn to her lips and blew a single, long note, which was repeated throughout the battlefield.

Amelia used her bow as best she could to cover the fairies' retreat and joined them in the village center. The crystals and chimes adorning the trees glittered and clinked like an orchestra warming up for the show of a lifetime. Hundreds upon hundreds of fairies hovered or roosted in the boughs around the warrior princess, waiting expectantly for whatever words of deliverance she might have.

"We cannot fight the Blight with sword and spear," Amelia announced. "It is too big and Romut is too powerful, but that does not mean we are defeated. We have one chance to win this war, and here we will make our final stand. Our instruments are useless against the Blight, but we are not defenseless. We still have one final weapon we can use, and it is the greatest one of all—spirit. We must dance and sing with everything we have. Let our voices carry a message to Romut and his Blight that we will not yield to his pestilence. This is our home, our lives, and he is not welcome here!"

Amelia began to sing and moved with the music she conjured up. The crystals hummed with her as the chimes added to the beat. Her song was not made of words but of hope and life.

The fairies picked up the wordless tune and danced with her, their voices and motions so perfectly synchronized they became one in spirit. The crystals burst into iridescent light, stabbing out at the demons diving toward them with rainbow-like lasers that cut them to pieces faster than they could advance.

The entire forest began to glow, and the radiance soon spread beyond the verdant borders and into the Blight. Where the brilliance destroyed the darkness, life began to bloom anew. The demons cried out in pain and tried to flee the expanding light.

Even Romut halted his rumbling advance and cast his arms up in a vain attempt to shield himself from the blaze. His black, oily flesh began to harden and crack. The fissures creeping across his body glowed until they erupted from within, shredding his existence and purging his foul taint from the land.

The fairies cheered as the light spread and the jungle slowly regrew. The damage the Blight had caused was horrific, but the land was healing, and life reasserted itself over death, as it invariably does.

Maala wrapped their savior in a fierce embrace. "You did it!"

Amelia smiled. "We all did it."

Felix and Ophelia took turns hugging her.

"We are going to throw such a party!" Ophelia said.

Amelia sighed. "I have to go back. My parents are probably freaking out right now."

Maala nodded and squeezed her hand. "We understand. Thank you, and know that you are always welcome."

"Don't worry, I'll be back," Amelia promised.

CHAPTER 13

A melia raced back to the elevator, praying she was able to return to her room before her parents got there. The elevator appeared before her, and she darted inside.

"Otis, we did it! We beat Romut!"

Otis smiled down at her. "I never doubted that you would. Where to now?"

Amelia sighed. "You better take me back to my room. Everyone is probably worried sick about me."

Otis' smile slipped from his face and he laid a gentle hand on Amelia's tiny shoulder. "I'm sorry, but that is the one place I can no longer take you."

Her question died on her lips as she understood what Otis meant. "But...I won. The warrior princess always wins."

"Yes, she does, and then she goes off to her next great adventure," Otis said with a smile tinged with sadness.

Butterflies filled Amelia's stomach as she thought about her parents. "Can I see them, just to say goodbye?"

"It's against the rules," Otis said before giving her a wink and a smile, "but some rules are made to be broken, aren't they?"

Otis pushed a button and the elevator glided into motion. The doors opened and Amelia could see her parents sitting in a waiting room. Her mom was weeping inconsolably in her dad's arms. Her dad's eyes were red but they no longer poured out tears, likely having run dry some time ago.

Amelia's bottom lip trembled. "They look so sad."

"Of course they are. They love you very much. The pain will fade with time, but their love for you never will."

Amelia fought back her tears. Warrior princesses did not cry, and for the first time in her life, she wished she were just a normal girl.

She raised her hand and curled her slender fingers. "Later, taters." She sighed and looked up at Otis' gentle face. "What do I do now?"

"Well, I could take you to your next adventure, or…"

"Or what?"

"I have been doing this for a long while, and Lilith and I have decided it's time for us to move on. I can't think of a better person to take over my job than you, if you would like to."

Amelia's eyes went wide. "You want me to run the elevator?"

"You could take it anywhere you want at any time. Even better, you get to take other brave and adventurous souls on journeys of their own. After all, the only thing better than being happy is bringing joy into someone else's life."

Amelia chewed her lip as she thought, despite knowing she had come to a decision the moment he made the proposal. "I'll do it!"

Otis chuckled and squeezed her shoulder. "I thought that would be your answer."

He pressed a button and the elevator spirited them away. The doors slid open a moment later to allow a stately, elderly woman to board. She and Otis could not have been more different. His skin was dark where hers was so pale she looked almost ghostly. Her dress was decades out of style but obviously of the highest quality and fashion for the era.

She stood poised, almost rigid, as she gripped a floral pastel handbag. The one thing she had in common with Otis was the absolute love and adoration in her smile when she looked upon the kindly elevator operator.

Her stern countenance softened when she smiled down at Amelia. "You must be Amelia. Otis has told me all about you."

Amelia returned the look and shook her white-gloved hand. "He told me about you too."

"I am glad Otis was able to finally find a suitable replacement. It was time for us both to move on."

"Are you ready for your first mission?" Otis asked.

Amelia snapped a sharp salute. "Where to, sir?"

Otis beamed at Amelia. "All the way to the top."

Amelia's eyes traveled over the controls and spotted a solitary button situated at the very top of the panel, its golden glow beckoning her to push it. She pressed the button and the elevator responded accordingly. Otis and Lilith stood with their arms entwined, gazing into each other's eyes the entire trip.

The car glided to a stop and the doors opened to reveal a park of unimaginable beauty and perfection. Cobbled pathways led through trees and manicured lawns where every blade of grass and each leaf adorning the trees looked to have been placed by the hand of a master artist.

Birds and butterflies flitted through the air; their colors impossibly brilliant to her eyes. People walked the paths, sat on benches, or strolled across the grass. Music filled the air, soft and undefinable yet clear and melodious.

Otis and Lilith stepped out of the elevator and onto one of the cobbled pathways. Otis' red operator's uniform turned a pristine white before her eyes. The couple looked back at the young girl staring from within the elevator and smiled, their aged faces young again. Although their wrinkles were gone, their eyes reflected the same love they had shared for a lifetime, a love that would continue for all eternity.

CHAPTER 14

Aaron trudged after his parents, pulling his Dragon Ball Z suitcase behind him. The wheels clacked against the marble floor every time it rolled over a seam in the polished stone slabs. His emaciated body made him appear younger, or at least smaller, than his eight years of age, but his haunted, hollowed eyes and loose skin gave him the appearance of a tiny old man.

He stopped in the middle of the hotel lobby while his parents went to the front desk to check in. Aaron adjusted the too-big baseball cap sitting loosely on his bald head and meandered closer to where a young woman in a hotel uniform was speaking to a small group of people.

"Welcome to the Grand Gloucester Hotel," the tour guide said. "The Grand Gloucester was built in 1908 by a wealthy industrialist named Rupert Bonet. His daughter inherited the hotel, along with his remaining fortune, when he died in 1932. Lilith Bonet spent the rest of her life in the hotel's penthouse suite where she became one of the most accomplished and highly regarded off-Broadway playwrights of her era.

"Despite the success of her expansive written works, it is said that Lilith never attended or even read so much as a single review of any of her plays, famously stating in a rare interview that she wrote for other people's enjoyment, not her own. In fact, she had one of the hotel's elevator operators cut any mention of her plays out of her daily newspaper before he delivered it."

The tour guide lowered her voice. "Rumor had it that she and the elevator operator, an African-American gentleman named Otis Garland, were secretly in love. Such a thing would have been quite a scandal for the period given her wealth and Otis' position, not to mention the deep racial divide of the time.

"While there was never any proof of their relationship, Otis was one of the last full-time elevator operators in the entire northeast.

She pointed to the elevator across the lobby. "Otis Garland remained at his post in that very elevator until his death in 1968. Perhaps it was no coincidence that Lilith passed away just three days later, unable or unwilling to live without her dear Otis. Some staffers and even guests claim to have heard the sound of scissors clipping in the elevator, and that Otis still brings her the newspaper to this very day. In a few minutes, I'll take you on a ride in Otis' elevator up to the museum where Lilith spent so many decades creating a lifetime of amazing plays."

"Aaron," his mother called out to him, "come on. Let's get to our room."

Aaron followed his parents to the elevator. "Can we go see the museum? The lady says it might be haunted."

"Maybe later. You look exhausted," she replied.

The elevator doors opened, and Aaron smiled at the pretty blonde girl standing in the back of the car as he stepped in.

"Hi, my name's Amelia. What's yours?" she asked as the doors slid shut.

"I'm Aaron."

His mom glanced down, a quizzical look on her face. "Who are you talking to?"

Amelia winked and pressed a finger to her pursed lips.

Aaron smiled up at his mother. "No one."

Amelia leaned close and whispered, "You're gonna love it here."

FROM THE AUTHOR

I hope you enjoyed this tale and will try my other works. Feel free to look me up on Facebook! You can also check me out on my website http://brockdeskins.com/ where I write serial fiction, free for your enjoyment, and answer questions!

Author page:
https://www.amazon.com/Brock-Deskins/e/B005M6VQ1O

Facebook:
https://www.facebook.com/brocksbooks/

Twitter:
@brockdeskins

PLEASE REVIEW MY BOOKS (Especially if you liked it). Customer reviews are the primary means of enticing others to purchase them. I am dependent upon the sales of my books to earn a living that will allow me to continue writing stories that I hope bring you some measure of entertainment. Thank you for your support.

OTHER BOOKS BY BROCK E. DESKINS

The Sorcerer's Path is an epic fantasy series.

The Sorcerer's Ascension: Torn from a life of comfort and luxury, his family destroyed by political intrigues and aspirations, a young boy must quickly grow into a man before the deadly streets of Southport devour him. Follow Azerick through a page-turning adventure that pits him against thieves, thugs, murderers, and men of power that will stop at nothing to achieve their goals.

Azerick must fight just to survive, but for him survival is not enough. A hunger to avenge the wrongs committed against him burns deep within. But that is not all that lies within the young man. There is a power waiting to be unleashed that may be the key to achieving the justice and security he seeks--if it does not destroy him first.

The Sorcerer's Torment: Azerick flees The Academy but quickly falls prey to powerful beings that use his skills and power for their own amusement. What these creatures do not understand is the power of the young sorcerer's will and the lengths he will go to for vengeance. Despite becoming a prisoner, Azerick finds his first true love, but can he keep it?

The Sorcerer's Legacy: Azerick has found himself a home and tries to settle down. He takes on an apprentice and tries to put all the death and desire for vengeance behind him. But when the Rook finds him, Azerick is once again pulled back into Ulric's schemes. Knowing that all he has worked toward and everyone close to him is in danger as long as these schemes are ongoing; Azerick decides to put an end to it, once and for all.

The Sorcerer's Vengeance: After narrowly avoiding being killed in his own bed by the land's most feared assassin, Azerick leaves his school behind to find out who sent him and to put an end to the threat once and for all. Azerick's search will take him to the very pits of the abyss and back to unleash hellish fury upon those that threaten him.

The Sorcerer's Scourge: With the siege broken and Ulric dead, Azerick can finally relax, study his magic, and run his school in peace. Unfortunately, Jarvin's reign is far from uncontested and the true usurper decides to make his move. Jarvin escapes with help from an unlikely source—a vampire named Landrin who still clings tenaciously to his own humanity. While Azerick and a large force from North Haven race to save the king in exile, evil forces are preparing to unleash a nightmare upon the kingdom that may well destroy them all.

The Sorcerer's Abyss: Now the master of the Fifth Circle of the abyss, Azerick is challenged by another demon lord for supremacy. Azerick must face this threat as well as his innermost demons, all the while searching for a way to escape his hellish prison.

Ellyssa fears she is going insane as she plagued by nightmares of her capture and enslavement. Deciding the key to saving herself lies in the total destruction of the object of her fears, she embarks on a crusade to find and kill the slaver, Captain Jake, and eradicate the slave trade.

Ellyssa's nightmares and battles spill out onto the streets of North Haven and gains the attention of The Academy. Fearing Azerick's school is turning out rogue wizards, The Academy decides to hunt down and destroy the rogue and place the school within their control.

The Sorcerer's Return: Azerick has come back from the abyss in order to try to unite all the races against the return of the old gods who seek to destroy them and subjugate the few they allow to survive a brutal purging. However, fighting ancient gods may be the least of his troubles as he battles to save a fractured kingdom, a brilliant son traveling a dark path, and the splintered soul of his own humanity.

The Sorcerer's Destiny: Brutally purged of his demonic influence, Azerick continues the struggle of uniting the kingdom to face the coming of the Scions, ancient gods banished by the mortal races during the Great Revolution two thousand years ago. The fallen gods' prison is crumbling, and Azerick is powerless to stop them from breaking free and enacting their cataclysmic vengeance upon the world.

The humans must ally with the other races in a final battle against impossible odds while their entire world crumbles to the ground and is trod beneath the feet of an unstoppable foe. How can they set aside their distrust of each other when they fear the very person trying to save them?

Rise of the Order: Banished to the abyss after helping defeat the Scions and saving the world from eternal darkness, Azerick languishes in perpetual misery as Lord of the Fifth Circle. The denizens of his hellish realm view him as a usurper and outsider. The chaotic creatures form an alliance with one goal in mind: destroy Azerick Giles, but Sharrellan stands in their way.

A powerful spell tears through the demonic planes, and when the dust settles, the dark goddess is nowhere to be found. It is up to Azerick to return her to her seat of power, but he has a price: return him to his mortal form and send him home.

Back home, a vast empire is on a crusade to conquer the world, and it has set its sights on Valeria. Their goal is to unite the world under a single banner, eradicate the spawn infestation unleashed by the Scions, and replace the gods who they feel have forsaken them with their mystical rulers.

Can Azerick save the dark goddess from the clutches of her demonic subjects and become mortal once again? Will he have the power to protect his people from The Order if he does?

Descent Into Chaos: The Order has arrived in force, and the fate of Valeria, and perhaps all the world, is poised to come under their iron-fisted control. Azerick and Daebian are forced to flee Southport and make a contentious alliance when King Miles capitulates to the invaders. Reduced to insurgent warfare, Azerick and his allies attempt to battle The Order's vastly superior forces in a series of hit and run strikes, but the enemy legions may not be his biggest threat.

Princess Sylvian Attar, daughter to The Order's godlike emperor and empress, has taken a personal interest in Azerick. Herself a powerful sorceress, Sylvian hunts Azerick in hopes of removing Valeria's legendary hero from the battlefield thus sapping her enemies' will to fight. Azerick decides there is but one course of action he can take against this unstoppable foe. It was time to inject a little chaos into The Order.

Brooklyn Shadows is a modern-day vampire tale. Full of action and snarky dialogue, Brooklyn Shadows is an enjoyable read for anyone who enjoys the supernatural underworld and butt-kicking vampires.

Shrouds of Darkness (Brooklyn Shadows Book 1) Leo Malone has been a vampire for the better part of the twentieth century. Once a prominent Sherriff (vampire cop), he now earns his living as a private eye and occasional bodyguard for anyone that requires some serious protection. Leo is hired by the daughter of a mob accountant who has gone missing.

The fact that her father is also a werewolf has Leo following a trail of grisly murders that will lead him through a web of intrigue and conspiracy involving his fellow vampires and the local werewolves that make New York their home, all the while trying to keep one particularly determined cop off his back and himself out of jail. Leo is not some pretty-boy vampire that all the girls ogle over, but a hard-eyed, remorseless killing machine who does not take crap from anyone.

Blood Conspiracy (Brooklyn Shadows Book 2): While dealing with the aftermath of the failed vampire council coup, Leo discovers that the modified Cure has fallen into the hands of a black ops government project designed to create vampiric super soldiers. When the inevitable happens, the off-book Homeland Security operation forcefully enlists Leo to help them resolve the situation. Worse yet, he has to work not only with an antagonistic werewolf named Meat, he is reunited with his hated creator, Lesile.

Primacy of Darkness (Brooklyn Shadows Book 3): Jack the Ripper, sadistic madman of old London, once thought long dead, has returned to New York in an effort to quench his thirst for blood and mayhem. When the city's vampire enclave finds itself insufficient to deal with a madman of Jack's caliber, Vincent, the enclave head, enlists Leo Malone to put the maniac down before he reveals the existence of vampires as he throws the city into the throes of chaos and terror. Leo soon finds that Jack is not the only monster with which he must contend. A ghost from his past has also seemingly crawled from its grave and seeks to put an end to him and the rest of his kind.

The Transcended Chronicles is the story of an outlandish young man as he goes from being a troublesome youth to one of the kingdom's greatest secret agents. Blessed (or cursed) with an amazing ability to both fight and abuse his body with every conceivable vice known to man, Garran Holt is either the kingdom's greatest hero or its biggest embarrassment.

<u>The Miscreant</u> (**The Transcended Chronicles Book 1**): Garran Holt is a troubled young man. Unable to tolerate his self-destructive ways, his mother sells him into indentured servitude as part of a work crew building King Remiel's new trade road. When mercenaries sent to disrupt the road's construction attack his work camp, Garran discovers an inner power capable of turning him into a warrior of unparalleled ability. When the leader of his work crew recognizes Garran as being one of the transcended (a fighter able to slip into the swifter currents of time), he is trained as an agent, one of the kingdom's elite spies. Crude, abrasive, and deeply committed to destroying himself with drugs, alcohol, and debauchery, Garran might be the kingdom's only hope against falling to The Guild, the powerful trade cartel bent on becoming the true and undisputed power in the land.

<u>The Agent</u> (**The Transcended Chronicles Book 2**): The Guild rules the kingdom through their puppet monarch, and Garran must race to save the last living heir to the throne before the powerful syndicate's assassins complete their extermination of anyone who could oppose them. Garran and Prince Adam Altena struggle to find allies in hopes of rescuing Adam's sister, who was forced to marry the usurper in order to prevent even the thought of rebellion, and raise an army

capable of defeating The Guild. With The Guild now in control of Anatolia's powerful army as well as their legion of mercenaries, their future is grim. How can a disreputable agent and a deposed prince convince their neighboring rulers to oppose The Guild, an organization that has had them cowed for decades?

Empire of Masks is an exciting and explosive new series that takes place in the world of Hedon and takes you across the land of Eidolan where ships sail through the skies and men and women wage war with magic, swords, muskets, and cannons.

Highlords of Phaer (Book one of Empire of Masks): Born a slave, descended of kings, Jareen Velarius just wants to provide the best life he can for his family, but Eidolan is a realm that challenges even the most stalwart of souls. Caught between his masters and those brave or foolish enough to strike against them, Jareen struggles to reconcile his role as a dutiful slave with that of a man who desires to be free. His goal: to return his people to a life stolen by the highlords more than a millennium ago.

Auberon Victore, sorcerer, alchemist, son of a powerful overlord, and Jareen's master, creates an alchemic compound he is certain will change the world; he just does not know how. Jareen sees it for the weapon that could break the sorcerers' iron grasp wrapped around the necks of every lowborn in the empire. It will change the world, but not in the way his master desires.

Across the Tempest Sea, a mighty storm has raged for a thousand years, keeping a terrible, long-forgotten enemy at bay, an enemy whose cruelty knows no bounds. Only the perpetual storm and their fear of the sorcerer highlords keep the Necrophages from returning to Eidolan and cloaking the empire in death and darkness. But the tempest is waning, and the dissidents' freedom may well come at the cost of their total destruction.

Nightbird: The Great Revolution ended the highlords' tyranny two hundred years ago, but the legacy of that epic war, and that of the principal architects' descendants, lives on. With the highlords' death and their taking magic, as it was once known, to their graves, Eidolan fell into a time of darkness and its cities lived in isolation. However, some people, dubbed arcanists, discovered a new form of magic and the airships returned to the skies, rejoining the cities in trade as well as conspiracy, but a new darkness, more dreadful and deadly than any they faced before, is coming.

Kiera is a fifteen-year-old nightbird, one of many who flit about after dark, stealing whatever they can find in order to survive. She lives on a derelict airship in the poorest part of the city with Wesley, a young man who plies his trade as an escort to wealthy older women, and his little brother Russel, an autistic savant who communicates only through sign but who could secretly be the most powerful techno-arcanist the empire has ever known. Deep in debt to the underlord Nimat, Kiera dives into evermore dangerous schemes that put her at the heart of a secret war that could spell the destruction of not just the city, but the very empire.

Kiera is caught in the center of several factions on the brink of war. When she can no longer tell friend from enemy, there is only one side she can trust—her own.

Mourningbird: A creature of darkness lurks in the shadows of Velaroth, wearing the skin of its victims, and grips the city in terror. Dorian, a Necrophage bent on sowing chaos and paving the way for his people's invasion, has declared war on the humans of Eidolan, and there appears to be no one capable of stopping him.

Kiera's world is shattered by those who hold power, and she is forced to seek an ally. The nightbird is coming into power of her own, but can she stay alive long enough to seize it? Russel's behavior has taken a turn for the worse, and his actions have drawn the attention of those who would use his amazing talents for their own gain…and everyone else's loss.

The battle for Velaroth, and perhaps the world, has begun. Who will win? Who will live to mourn the dead? Will there be anything left for the victor to claim as their prize?

Standalone books

The Portal is a fun and exciting story of some less than popular teenagers that accidentally open a portal to a mystical land during one of their role-playing games. Drew, a dour and anti-establishment teenager, is pulled through and captured by evil creatures lying in wait on the other side. Now it is up to his friends and older brother to rescue him, but who will rescue Drew's captors from him?

Amelia (Battle for Ardentia): Amelia is a precocious, ten-year-old girl with a powerful imagination. In her alter-ego guise of a demi-goddess warrior princess, Amelia fights against a powerful demonic sorcerer named Romut and his horde of monsters in a never ending series of battles to protect the people of her imaginary world. However, the true battle strikes home when Amelia is diagnosed with a brain tumor. Now Amelia must fight not just the evil living in her imagination, but for her very life.

ABOUT THE AUTHOR

Brock Deskins was born in a small town located in rural Oregon. At age twenty, he joined the army and served as an M1A1 tank crewman, dental specialist, and computer analyst. While in the military, he became an accomplished traveler, husband, and father of three wonderful children. His military career completed, attended college to brush up on his skills as a computer analyst and gain new skills as a writer. Brock received his degree in computer networking and is now devoting his full time and limited attention span to writing.

BIBLIOGRAPHY

THE SORCERER'S PATH
The Sorcerer's Ascension
The Sorcerer's Torment
The Sorcerer's Legacy
The Sorcerer's Vengeance
The Sorcerer's Scourge
The Sorcerer's Abyss
The Sorcerer's Return

The Sorcerer's Destiny
Rise of the Order
Descent Into Chaos

BROOKLYN SHADOWS
Shrouds of Darkness
Blood Conspiracy

THE TRANSCENDED CHRONICLES
The Miscreant
The Agent

EMPIRE OF MASKS
Highlords of Phaer
Nightbird
Mourningbird

OTHER BOOKS BY BROCK E. DESKINS
The Portal
Amelia: Battle for Ardentia

Curious about other Crossroad Press books? Stop by our website:
http://crossroadpress.com
We offer quality writing
in digital, audio, and print formats.

Subscribe to our newsletter on the website homepage and receive a
free eBook.